Joseph Hatton

The Tallants of Barton

A tale of fortune and finance - Vol. 1

Joseph Hatton

The Tallants of Barton
A tale of fortune and finance - Vol. 1

ISBN/EAN: 9783337344054

Printed in Europe, USA, Canada, Australia, Japan

Cover: Foto ©Andreas Hilbeck / pixelio.de

More available books at **www.hansebooks.com**

THE

TALLANTS OF BARTON.

A Tale of Fortune and Finance.

BY

JOSEPH HATTON,

AUTHOR OF "BITTER SWEETS: A LOVE STORY;" "AGAINST THE STREAM,"
ETC., ETC.

"The wheel of Fortune turns incessantly round, and who can say within himself,
I shall to-day be uppermost?"—*Confucius.*

IN THREE VOLUMES.

VOL. I.

LONDON:
TINSLEY BROTHERS, 18, CATHERINE ST., STRAND.
1867.

CONTENTS.

---◆---

TALLANTS OF BARTON.

CHAPTER I.

IN THE SHADOW OF BERNE HILLS.

BARTON HALL is a conspicuous feature of the
landscape in the smiling Vale of Avonworth, and
it stands beneath the shadow of Berne Hills.
Built of white stone, and in the Italian style of
architecture, it has the appearance of a modern
mansion removed from Kensington Palace Gardens, and planted amongst the rare scenery of
this beautiful western district of the Midlands.

All that wealth and taste can do to make the
house generally worthy of the site has been
lavished upon it, inside and out. It is furnished
with everything that is costly and comfortable,

with ornaments and articles of *vertu* from all parts of the earth.

A long gravelly drive leads up to the principal entrance, which is cut off from the park with iron fencing and chains. On the other side of the house there are conservatories of flowers and extensive gardens. Behind, at a short distance, there is stabling for many horses, shut out from view by shrubs and young trees.

In front of the house a smooth tract of mossy lawn ends in a sunk fence; and beyond lies the park, skirted by green fields, which mount up the Berne Hills and lose themselves in the foliage of oaks, and elms, and larches.

Here and there on the lawn are clumps of young aspiring cedars, silver birch trees, ash plants, and sycamores, hemmed round about with rims of white creepers and luxuriant mosses. In "Gems of the Poets," pictorially adorned by Laydon, you will find a fanciful illustration of Gray's well-known lines:

" Full many a gem of purest ray serene
The dark, unfathom'd caves of ocean bear."

In the foreground there is a leafy vignette of
exotic and other plants and trees sprouting up
from an island-rock. Turn the water into grass,
and replace the tall cocoa-nut trees with a
couple of silver birches, and you have one of the
Barton Hall lawn groups; for the place is so
completely "shut out from the rude world" and
the easterly and northern winds, that the climate
is more like southern France than western England, and vegetation flourishes there nearly all
the year round.

Close by the principal lodge-entrance to the
park lies a clear deep lake, fed by a stream
from the Berne Hills, and the rendezvous of
innumerable wild and tame water-fowl.

Few places in broad England can compare with
this modern house and grounds. The sunsets
are more beautiful here than anywhere else in
all this western land. The twilights are full of
yellows, and delicate neutral tints, and shifting

lights. And the mists that float about those Berne Hills, like angel shadows! and the gentle rains that follow them, filling the air with a thousand mixed perfumes, and brightening the greens and browns in the landscape,—they might make an artist frantic with delight.

In rain or sunshine, in winter or summer, Barton Hall, beneath the shadow of Berne Hills, is always beautiful. In evening sunsets, with the red light on its great flashing windows, and a tinge of gold on the vane of its Italian tower, you might take it for the romantic retreat of a southern king rather than the home of a merchant prince of Old England.

Christopher Tallant was to all intents and purposes a self-made man. He had begun life in a humble capacity in the counting-house of some great works in the north of England, where so many men of position and influence have made their way upwards from minor posts.

They look more at a boy's talents than at his friends in those busy hives of industry northwards. No matter how highly a young fellow may be connected, he has no position without ability in these busy districts.

A rare practical race, these said northerners —a race to be brought up amongst, studied for example's sake. As a class they do not possess the refinements of manner and speech of the southern races of England, and they do not count so much upon etiquette. They are rough like their north-east winds, but genial as their own firesides.

Their rivers are black with coal washings, and the banks thereof are crowded with great works, from which blazing furnaces, and forges, and flashes of sudden flame, cast ruddy reflections upon the sullen tide. Their fields are covered with pit-heaps, and iron works, and lime-kilns, and blasting cupolas. But here and there, in out-of-the-way places, you come upon romantic woods, and running streams, and rocky glens.

A wonderful land the north countrie, the seat of great enterprises, and the home of strong-limbed, strong-willed, clear-headed men; one would rather some of them had softer manners, but for our country's good we can afford to sacrifice that if only in deference to their active brains and their inborn love of enterprise.

It was in the north, we say, where Mr. Christopher Tallant began life, and where the key-note of his career may be said to have been struck; but as a young man he had lived in the south-west of England, and had mastered the leading principles of trade and commerce in several great private and public works. He had proved himself an adept at legislative finance, at devising and carrying out great schemes; and at a comparatively early age he had raised himself to a position of commercial distinction and opulence.

He had been twice married. His first union was an unhappy one. It was altogether a mysterious marriage, which had puzzled and astonished his friends at the time, as well it might; for without the smallest warning the young fellow had returned from a short visit to London with a handsome, dashing woman, whom he introduced as his wife. At this time he was manager of the Vulcan Forge Works on the Avon, twenty miles on the other side of a famous western city, and he had the *entrée* to very respectable society.

It was some time before the little local coterie forgave his sudden introduction of the unknown London wife. In a very short time he had reason to repent his rashness and folly. His wife indulged in all kinds of extravagance; she led the local fashions, she indulged in fast flirtations which set all the gossips in the neighbourhood upon her; finally, an unwomanly passion for drink set in, and after a few years of wretchedness she died, leaving behind her one child, a son, who will make a prominent figure in this history.

The poor woman's misconduct had but little impeded her husband's worldly advances; he secured shares in several important patents; he became director of one or two companies; and started as an iron merchant on his own private account. At one time he held as his own property half the iron bars of a whole district. This was during a strike, after a period of great depression, and just before a time of sudden and unexpected activity.

Well, by-and-by, in the course of half-a-dozen years, the iron merchant married again, and took his wife home to that beautiful country residence near Severntown, and beneath the shadow of Berne Hills. He had only purchased the estate the year before his marriage.

His second wife, whom he had loved with a fervency characteristic of his earnest character, was the daughter of a nobleman, and an exceedingly handsome and lovable woman.

She died in giving birth to her first child, who, like her half-brother, is one of the leading characters in this story.

The death of his second wife had been a great affliction to Christopher Tallant. It was many months before he could bring himself even to look at his child. Travel and change of scene, lapse of time, increased ardour in business occupations, and new hopes, at length softened down his great sorrow, and enabled him to take his place in the great world calmly, and as became a man of his station and influence. His new hopes centred round his only son, who was a lad about eight years old when the merchant's greatest trouble came upon him.

The boy exhibited considerable native talent. He was a smart, well-looking, promising fellow, full of life and spirits and courage. Before he was ten years old his father clung to him like a forlorn hope, and centred in him schemes of future power and greatness. The name of Tallant had of late years become famous in the world of trade and money, and the name should be per- petuated in this son with honour and distinction. This was the happiness which, it seemed to the merchant, Fate had decreed he should have at last.

Such, briefly, is the outline of Mr. Tallant's history. We introduce him to our readers some two and twenty years after the death of his second wife,—a man over fifty years of age. At the time when we make his acquaintance he is Chairman of the great Meter Iron Works Company, a director of two of the principal railway companies, and a shareholder in many extensive city schemes.

Once a week he was to be found at the London offices of the Meter Works at Westminster, and he usually returned from London the same day. You could not have mistaken him for anything but a shrewd, conscientious man of business if you had known him. He was above the middle height, and usually wore a black shooting-coat, fitting the body tightly, and with pockets at the side; shepherd's plaid trowsers, and a black velvet waistcoat. His hair was grey, and his face cleanly shaven. He had a quick, discerning eye, and withal a genial expression of countenance; for, though he had not forgotten the past, Time had been good to him, as it is good to other sufferers who have lost dear ones from their homes, and had comforted him with the affection of his children. He bore an excellent character for kindness, integrity, and honour; but he was known at the same time to be a man of unbending pride.

He was proud of his name, of his wealth, of his son, of his house, of his grounds, of his farms, of his estates; proud of everything. And to a certain extent it was a laudable pride, for his riches were the result of his own ability and industry. He felt, with a certain acknowledgment of the bounty of Providence, that he had made them all himself. He might have thanked God a little more for his worldly success and been none the less happy, and certainly more grateful; but it was his pride that he had worked his way up, from the lowest rung of the ladder, and that he stood on the top of it with safety.

Everything he had was better than anything anybody else had; he would have it so, and yet he was a kindly, courteous sort of man, whom you might have had pleasure in visiting. His pride of wealth would crop up now and then; but his wines were superb, his *cuisine* everything that could be desired, the views from his windows magnificent, his pictures modern and by the best moderns, his books modern and in glorious bindings, and his daughter—there was nothing more sweet to look upon in all the Avonworth valley, or beneath the Berne Hill shades, than the merchant's only daughter.

CHAPTER II.

INTRODUCES THE READER TO THE MERCHANT'S
SON AND DAUGHTER.

Do you know Dicksee's picture of " Miranda ?"
It was exhibited at the Royal Academy a few
years ago. There are copies of it in the Strand
and Regent Street picture-shops.

It is a fair, sweet, *spirituel* face, full of inquiring love and innocence—a frank, open face, set
off with a heavy wealth of bright brown hair—a
sunny face, with red, parted lips, and all the pure
soul of woman in the deep blue eyes.

When first we saw that picture, we could not,
"for the life of us," think where we had seen the
earthly model of it. It haunted us for days; we
dreamt about it; we bought the best copy we
could procure; and at length, with the picture

lying beside us, carefully packed, on the seat of a Great Western Railway carriage, a London purchase for our country library, we remembered Phœbe Tallant.

It hangs before us whilst we write, with all the story of the life of her whom it so much resembles mapped out in our mind.

'Perhaps Phœbe Tallant was not quite so pretty as Mr. Dicksee's picture, but she was as near an approach to it as one is likely to meet with once in a dozen years.

Occasional visitors at Barton Hall from London were in raptures with the bright, fair girl; and one or two young fellows had gone home desperately in love with her; but none of them dared hardly to think of their love in presence of Mr. Tallant: not that the merchant said much about Phœbe, not that she seemed to be on such affectionate terms with him as might have been expected; but he was proud of her beauty, proud of her accomplishments. And, moreover, it was shrewdly anticipated that Miss Tallant would not have anything like the dowry which the daughter of so wealthy a father ought to have; for the merchant was all engrossed in his heir.

Richard Tallant, who was destined by the old man for such a store of riches, was a dark, dashing young fellow, of five or six and twenty, when we first make his acquaintance—some half-a-dozen years older than his half-sister Phœbe.

He had been an Eton boy, had graduated at Oxford, and travelled through Europe and Asia.

He had already spent enough money recklessly, foolishly, ay, and wickedly, to have produced an annuity of at least a thousand a year. He was professedly one of the managing directors of the Meter Works, and resided in London to take the metropolitan and continental business of the company.

When his father complained of his enormous expenditure (which was very seldom, by the way), Richard Tallant alluded to his position in the world, his education, and his habits.

At Oxford he had been a don, not of learning,

but of fashion; kept his hunters and his mail phaeton, and made many a scion of the old aristocracy envy the mushroom son of iron and railway debentures.

"You have given me every indulgence; you have bred me up in the hot-bed of luxury; I am just fresh from a European tour, where I travelled like a prince, to finish my college education, and now you expect me to pull in," Richard would say, sitting astride one of the heavy mahogany chairs in the Westminster managerial room, and looking over the back of it at his father.

"I should not care, Dick, if you would only do the work of your office, as well as draw the salary," Mr. Tallant would remark.

"Come, now, my dear governor, have you not told me you have enough invested to enable me to live like a prince all my life?"

"I may have been weak enough to say so; but I calculated upon your doing something towards keeping the money coming in."

" You didn't want me, you said, to be waiting, like some heirs, for your death, and then reckoning upon living in style; you would rather I had my fill of life, and see me enjoy it in your own days. Come now, father, you know you have said so," said Richard, twirling his moustache, and tapping his patent-leather boot with a riding-whip.

" I fear I had not my usual foresight about me when I did say so," said Mr. Tallant.

And he said truly; but having risen by hard work himself, and sprung from a comparatively humble position, Mr. Tallant was one of those men who like to see their children in the other extreme, and who, never having been within the pale of college and aristocratic life, believe, and truly, that, to be a leader therein, a merchant's son must let his money fly freely, and like a prince indeed.

He had given his son a free rein. When first Richard went to Oxford, he had been snubbed by a young lord, and an epigram had been levelled at him, the point of which turned upon his name and origin; he was called the produce of fifty talents of silver invested in iron.

When Richard told his father this, the great merchant snapped his fingers, and said he could buy up all the Oxford lords in a heap, and, turning cleverly round upon their lordships, in reply to the epigrammatic hit at his son's origin, he said,

"Never mind them, Dick; there's as good blood in your veins as there is in any of theirs; it may not come from a swell who plundered the Saxons at the time of the Norman Conquest, or mixed in the vices of licentious courts; there is no dishonour in it, and it has to be proved yet whether to spring from merchant princes of England is not the highest of all descent."

"Bravo," said Mr. Richard Tallant; "why, father, you speak like an orator. That hit about the merchant princes would drive half-a-dozen hustings mad."

Mr. Tallant had warmed up, and was angry; he paid no attention to his son's comment; he only saw before him some "stuck up" aristocrat sneering at his name and origin.

"Look here, Dick," he continued, producing a blank cheque, "fill that up in the presence of these aristocratic snobs, and show them what the Tallants can do."

This was surely putting too much of power and revenge into the hands of a young man naturally frivolous and overbearing, and it no doubt influenced, in a great measure, his future career.

One would have given Mr. Christopher Tallant credit for more real worldly wisdom than this; he could, perhaps, have borne "the proud man's contumely" himself; he might have shrugged his shoulders, and sneered at it, with a consoling thought about his wealth; he might have said to himself, "Ah, never mind, I could buy you up, stick and stone" (for he was weak, you see, on this point); but he would not have protested and been demonstrative: contempt would have been his answer, and, in the midst of his commercial cares, he would have speedily forgotten the inane taunt. To have his son treated with indifference, to see him taunted with his origin, by men who had nothing but their ancestors to boast about; this was a different thing altogether, and he chafed at it, and was angry indeed.

His pride was shocked. The feeling that he could buy everything was shaken. He was not accustomed to crosses, except such as his wealth or his energy could overcome; and his sense of injured honour, too, was touched.

"I would not have you do anything that is mean, Dick; there is nothing mean in being generous and open-handed; and there are two powers, it appears, at Oxford,—money and blood; don't be afraid to hold your own; you have no reason to be ashamed of your birth, and you can make them ashamed of their poverty, the sneaks! Don't spare them one jot, Dick; punish them, and show them what talents of silver invested in iron can do—the miserable sneaks!"

Thus all the merchant's practical wisdom and his just pride were thrown to the winds; but he is not the only man of his class who, chafing at the arrogance of "gentle blood," has sought revenge on Society at the shrine of Mammon, and obtained nothing in return but "a crown of golden sorrow."

CHAPTER III.

BRINGS US TO THE HALL FARM, WHERE THE
READER MAKES THE ACQUAINTANCE OF THE
SOMERTONS AND A CERTAIN LANDSCAPE
PAINTER.

IT lay on the western border of the park, and
comprised about eight hundred acres of arable and
pasture land.

The buildings were red brick, with white
dressed corner stones and facings. There were
model cow-houses, cattle-sheds, piggeries, barns,
corn-lofts, and poultry pens, that would have
satisfied even Mr. Mechi's critical eye. An agricultural writer of considerable repute had, in truth,
written an essay upon these model buildings, and
it had been printed in an important agricultural
and scientific review; for there were no better
arranged buildings in the country.

Mr. Tallant, you know, would have the best of everything, and his bailiff encouraged him in having all the best things at his farm. There were carts from Crosskill, ploughs from Ransomes, thrashing-machines from Clayton and Shuttleworth, reapers from America, clod-crushers, drills, rakes, hoes, harrows, and other implements from Banbury, Lincoln, Beverley, Worcester, Yorkshire, and Bristol.

Mr. Tallant had built these model farm-buildings himself. The Hall Farm had been an especial feature of the estate when he purchased it, but the buildings did not come up to his notions, and the result is before us.

Mr. Tallant brought all his commercial experience to bear upon the cultivation and management of the land. His bailiff, Mr. Luke Somerton, had been a Lincolnshire lord's right hand in the management of a great farm on the Wolds, and he was the very man of all others to enter into Mr. Tallant's idea of looking upon a farm in the same light as he would a manufactory.

The merchant maintained that good land would, in a very few years, amply repay a man for all he put into it; and Mr. Somerton was a thorough-going disciple of high cultivation. He had studied agricultural chemistry under a professor, and Mr. Tallant often said it was quite a treat to chat with him about Liebig's theories, the value of agricultural statistics, tenant right, and leases. Richard Tallant did not agree with his father, and thought Luke Somerton's talk a good deal of it " rot :" not that the bailiff cared for Mr. Richard's opinion, or feared his father's.

Luke Somerton was quite a gentleman in his way. He was a younger son of a Lincolnshire squire, and had been brought up to agriculture as a profession. He came to the Barton Hall Farm with Mr. Tallant, and he was likely to remain there as long as Mr. Tallant lived; for he was not only a scientific farmer, but he farmed profitably, and Mr. Tallant said that was what few amateur gentlemen farmers could say for their bailiffs in that district.

The farm-house was a substantial, handsome residence, surrounded with a prettily laid out garden, with shrubs and trees all scrupulously dwarfed and pruned. Hard by, and adjacent to the farm-buildings, was the stack yard, and beyond were fields, mostly grass, with low fences and white gates.

Mr. Somerton was married, and had three children,—two sons and a daughter. His firstborn had left home when he was fifteen as an apprentice on board a merchant ship, which sailed from London for Bombay. The vessel had been spoken once, and had never been heard of afterwards; so Frank had long been mourned as lost, and there remained the bailiff, his daughter Amy, a girl about the age of Miss Tallant, and a son, Paul, three years younger.

Luke Somerton's married life had not been a happy one. His wife had accepted his hand mainly out of spite, after she had angled unsuccessfully for his eldest brother. She was a proud disappointed woman ; but a good housewife nevertheless, and Luke, by dint of perseverance, had successfully combated her overbearing disposition; so that though they could not be said to live happily and affectionately, as man and wife should do, they never had noisy open brawls and quarrels, as some couples have. If they sneered at each other and maintained opposite opinions on almost any given subject, they very rarely had loud disputes, and never passed a day without speaking to each other. They were opposed on principle; but Mrs. Somerton always managed to conclude her bickerings with something like overtures of reconciliation, which Luke accepted for what they were worth, and "tided over with," until the next fencing bout came on.

Mrs. Somerton had been a handsome woman—a blonde—and might have continued handsome had she cultivated kindness of heart as well as her husband cultivated wheat. Hers was a nice face spoiled by a nasty temper. She was a fine woman, above the middle height, and there were little streaks of red upon her cheeks such as you see on the sunny side of a winter apple. There were lines about her mouth which disappointment and pride had placed there, during eighteen years of sourness and vexation of spirit. She was well mated so far as appearances went.

Her husband looked a thorough son of the soil, a tall, well-built, florid, intelligent, business-like Lincolnshire farmer, such as you will meet in the capacity of judge at country agricultural shows.

Their son Paul was at a boarding-school, and when this story begins, just about commencing life as a clerk in Mr. Tallant's London offices.

His sister Amy was at home, and spent half her time at the Hall with Miss Tallant, who treated her very much as a sister.

Amy was not at all like the picture of Miranda. She was several shades darker than Miss Tallant, and neither a brunette nor a blonde ; but she had a large black piercing eye, which looked at you from beneath gracefully-arched eyebrows. She was not so round as Phœbe ; but her figure was supple, and well defined. Her mouth and chin were full of graceful curves, and her hair was bound closely to her head, setting off a pair of small white ears that gave a high character to the face. She was a well-bred, high-spirited girl, and accomplished too; for she had not only been fairly educated at her father's expense, but she had had the benefit of much of the tuition which Miss Tallant had received, not only from a clever resident governess but from professors who came at intervals to Barton Hall.

Amongst the latter was one Mr. Arthur Phillips, who taught Miss Tallant drawing, and as he will figure rather prominently in this romance, we will introduce him at once, and tell you what he was like and all about him. He was a rising young artist who resided in the county town, though he might have made a successful position in London.

"I wonder you don't go to town," many persons would say to him; and his reply would be in effect,

"Why should I? I don't care for London, and I like the country. I can go to town whenever I think proper, and the dealers will buy my pictures whether I go or not. What I get for them, and the few pupils I have in the county, give me enough for all my requirements, and enable me to study quietly and leisurely."

But there was another reason why Arthur Phillips preferred the country, and that was a reason, which you may guess, for constant visits to the vale of Berne, beyond his desire to study the foliage of the district, and the lights and shadows of the Berne hills, and the beautiful skies above.

It is true that many of his best sketches were transcriptions of the varied bits of landscape in this district ; and he said he had never thoroughly understood Cuyp, Both and Ruysdael, Salvator Rosa, Wilson and Gainsborough, until he knew Berne valley in storm and sunshine, in spring and summer. He was never tired of painting Berne trees and Berne mosses, and the dealers bought these little sketchy bits almost as readily as they would now buy similar things by Birket Foster.

Mr. Phillips was an earnest lover of art; if he had not been a painter he would have been a poet. There was poetry in all his works, the true poetry of nature; and he was as well up in the principles and beauties of poetry as he was in chiaroscuro and perspective.

Nature had given him a mind worthy of the most perfect exterior, but she had denied him many of those charms of person which mostly delight the eye and captivate the heart of woman. He was under the ordinary height, a thin figure, with long black hair, and dark eyes set deeply in a face notable for sharply cut features. The expression was that of a thinker, and his manner nervous and retiring.

Mrs. Somerton had a great objection to Mr. Phillips.

"I don't think his continually lurking about here bodes any good to those girls," she said to her husband, over tea, as Mr. Phillips passed by, with his sketch book under his arm.

"Nonsense," said Mr. Somerton, laughing. "You

don't think either of the girls will fall in love with an undersized whipper-snapper like Mr. Phillips ?"

"There's no knowing what poor silly women will fall in love with," said Mrs. Somerton, with a sneer.

"No, nor men either, for the matter of that, dame, if you want to argue the point," Luke replied, defiantly.

Mrs. Somerton, thus challenged, declined to pick up the gauntlet which she had so often before accepted. She was bent upon talking about Mr. Arthur Phillips.

"I don't think Amy would be fool enough to be led away by his poetry and pictures, and fine speeches and things; but Miss Tallant's soft enough for anything, and I wonder Mr. Tallant has that fellow continually about the place."

"God bless us !" said Mr. Somerton, his honest face lighting up with a genial smile of amusement; "why, do you think Miss Tallant, with her beautiful face, and her equally beautiful dowry, is going to throw herself away upon poor little Phillips ?"

"Why not ? He writes poetry, and paints all sorts of nonsense, and talks like lackadaisical lovers talk in books; and I'm sure that's the sort of thing that Miss Tallant's flashy education has taught her to admire. Why didn't her father let her go into London society ? Why doesn't she go to town for the season, and be a reigning beauty, as she might be? That's the sort of education she should have had, and then she might have married a duke," Mrs. Somerton said, with warmth.

"Why, you're quite excited about it," said Mr. Somerton; "I've not seen your eyes sparkle so since I don't know when."

"I hate to see such namby-pambyism," went on Mrs. Somerton. "When a girl's got a pretty face, a graceful manner, and plenty of money, she ought to take her place and marry a gentleman, not be buried alive in a stucco palace, with a half-gentleman, half-farmer, half-ironfounder father, a sneaking governess, and an ugly, romantic little painter."

"Well, well, wife, it is no business of ours, and if it was, I don't think there's any foundation for alarm. Besides, your ambition ought to be satisfied if young Hammerton, as you say pays more delicate attentions to Amy than he does to Miss Tallant. But Master Hammerton must mind his eye; I'd break every bone in his body if he offered an insult to Amy."

"Young Hammerton!" said Mrs. Somerton, with an affected sneer. "Do you think I'm vain and silly enough to think the daughter of a farm-bailiff has any chance of catching the next heir to an earldom, for her husband?"

"A farm-bailiff! Why such emphasis on farm-bailiff, Mistress Somerton? There may be as good blood in the veins of a farm-bailiff as there is in a Hammerton."

Mrs. Somerton's lip curled with a pitying, patronising expression, that put her husband into a towering passion; a most unusual circumstance.

"Damn it!" he exclaimed, rising from his seat, "a Somerton is as independent a man any day; there was never one of the race that didn't always pay twenty shillings in the pound, and but wouldn't fell a lord if he spoke a light word of any of their women: and, by heaven, I consider myself as good a man as any Hammerton, dead or living."

"There, there, Luke; now don't get into a passion," said Mrs. Somerton, trying to speak soothingly, and like an injured woman, who had not given the slightest cause for passion to anybody in all her life.

"What's the meaning of all this, Sarah? There's something at the bottom of it."

"Only a friendly gossip between man and wife; but that's such a novelty in this house, is it not?"

"I have had enough experience to tell me that a friendly gossip like this is not meant for nothing, Sarah," said Luke, thrusting his hands into his pockets, and pacing about the room.

Whether there was anything "at the bottom of it," or not, did not further transpire at that moment, by reason of the Hon. Lionel Hammerton himself dismounting from his horse at the gate beyond the garden, and walking up to Mr. Somerton's door.

CHAPTER IV.

THE offices of Mr. Tallant and the Meter Works were at Westminster, in a magnificent newly erected block of buildings not far from the Houses of Parliament. They comprised the whole suite of apartments on the ground-floor, with a board-room above.

On the heavy swinging mahogany doors at the entrance were two thick brass plates, on one of which was engraven "Meter Iron Works Company," and on the other "Christopher Tallant."

The establishment was fitted up in the best possible style, with mahogany desks; the counting-house was very much like a bank, the whole of the monetary business of the great company, as well as that of Mr. Tallant, being conducted in town. Behind the counting-house was Mr. Christopher Tallant's room, and that of his son Richard.

Mr. Tallant's room was plainly but well furnished, and was only occupied once a week; but Mr. Richard's room was fitted up in the highest style of office magnificence, like a gentleman's library. There was a thick velvet-pile carpet upon the floor, a massive carved mahogany table in the centre of the room; several ponderous chairs with morocco seats; a quaint arm-chair stood before a writing-pad near the table. Where there were no book-shelves there were pictures of engines, and iron bridges, and curious girders, and wheels, in ponderous frames; and thick cloth curtains draped the two windows which looked into the street.

The offices were famous amongst men in the iron trade, and once or twice Mr. Tallant began to think they were getting a name politically; for several deputations had waited upon him there soliciting him to come forward for various boroughs at general elections.

But Mr. Christopher Tallant always said his ambition did not lie that way. Some day perhaps his son Dick might like to go into the House, and if he did, why go he should of. course; but there was plenty of time to think about that; and so the deputations retired, wishing, in most cases, that there were not plenty of time to think about that, for there was gold indeed at the back of Christopher Tallant.

"By gad, you amuse me," said Mr. Shuffleton Gibbs, a college acquaintance of Mr. Richard Tallant's, looking at the pictorial treasures of the room through an eye-glass. "To think of your going in for engines and machines, with idiotic cranks, and all that sort of thing. 'Pon my soul, it's too funny."

And Mr. Shuffleton Gibbs turned round, showed Mr. Richard Tallant his teeth, and said "haw, haw." That was the way Mr. Gibbs laughed: that was how he laughed at Oxford, when a broken-hearted girl appealed to his sense of honour; that was how he laughed when he won two thousand pounds at Loo from a college friend, who said he was ruined, and threatened to throw himself into the Isis; that was how he laughed under all circumstances.

"One must put a sign of some sort up," said Mr. Richard Tallant, twirling his moustache, and stretching his legs under the big library table. "What will you take, Shuff?"

"Anything you intend taking yourself, old boy; you are a pretty good judge; I'll trust to your sense of what a fellow's morning draught should be," said Mr. Gibbs, grinning again, and saying "haw, haw" as before.

Mr. Tallant, junior, struck a gong upon the table, and a sober-looking old man in a dark livery obeyed the summons.

"Sherry, Thomas," said Mr. Richard.

Thomas taking up a bunch of keys from the table, unlocked a cupboard by the fireplace, and carefully uncorked a dusty, black looking bottle, and set it before Mr. Tallant's only son, with a couple of richly cut glasses.

Mr. Shuffleton Gibbs took a seat by the window, commended the wine as he drank it, and criticised any woman who chanced to pass on the other side of the street. He was not a beauty himself that he should be so critical of the looks of others. He had weak eyes, and shaky legs, a short cough, and a narrow chest. His enemies said he wore stays, and slept in gloves, to improve his figure and whiten his hands, which were naturally red, like his face, that was powdered after the manner of women. He was a man of fashion nevertheless, and had sprung of a noble stock; but the race flickered its last in him, and the estates had been divided by Jews in his grandfather's time.

It was considered a daring thing to be hand and glove with Gibbs at Oxford, a dangerous and a delightful thing; for he was known to be the fastest man of his college, and he had been the ring-leader in everything wicked for years. He made himself Mr. Tallant's champion when that gentleman was epigrammatically assailed, and ever afterwards constituted himself boon companion to the iron prince.

There was a rumour that Mr. Shuffleton Gibbs was compelled to leave college when he did on account of some offence committed against the regulations of the establishment; whether this was true or not, he left Oxford suddenly, and with no other honour than that of being the fastest man who had ever led a gown and town row, or hunted down a citizen's daughter.

"You'll be at the club to-night, of course," Mr. Gibbs said, swinging his eye-glass round, and admiring the perfect fit of a pair of new boots.

"Yes," said Mr. Richard, "shan't be able to come before dinner; going to dine with a friend at seven."

Mr. Gibbs showed his teeth, and said "haw, haw."

"Will join you by ten," Mr. Richard continued,

smiling, and holding his empty glass between himself and the light to catch its diamond-like sparkles in the sun.

"What's *your* little game to-night, then," inquired Mr. Tallant, junior.

"Nothing, nothing; a bit of quiet Loo and a cigar. Young Hammerton is to join us by-and-by."

"What, Earl Verner's brother?" Mr. Richard inquired, with more than ordinary interest.

"The same—the paternal seat is near Barton Hall, you know."

"Rather," said Mr. Richard. "He'll be deuced rich when the earl hops the twig; he is considerably older than Lionel and very shaky, they say; he often rides over to the Berne district. The governor says he likes to talk farming to the bailiff at the Hall Farm."

"Gad bless me!" exclaimed Mr. Gibbs. "Are there any gals about?"

"There is one, old fellow, and a remarkably fine girl, too; but her mother's a she-wolf, and her father!—why, Shuffy, he'd double you up with one hand and throw you into the road, if you put your nose into his place; he'd smell you out in no time;" and Mr. Richard Tallant laughed aloud at his lively picture of Mr. Gibbs's imaginary discomfiture.

Mr. Shuffleton Gibbs bit his lip before he grinned and said "haw, haw" this time; and it was a little while before he had time to say, "Haw, what an infernally powerful savage he must be."

Mr. Richard Tallant was, and had been for some time, of great pecuniary value to Mr. Shuffleton Gibbs, who not only sponged upon the iron prince, but fleeced him at cards, and assisted at all his extravagances. Had it been otherwise, he would have resented the tone and manner of Mr. Tallant's description of his perfect helplessness in the hands of Luke Somerton.

"You may laugh, Shuff, but by Jove it's true; so take timely warning, and if ever you should go down to Barton Hall mind how you look at Amy Somerton."

Mr. Tallant, senior, it would seem, had no liking for Mr. Shuffleton Gibbs, and he had privately intimated to his son that he would rather that gentleman were not amongst the friends whom he introduced to Barton Hall.

"If ever I go to Barton Hall!" said Mr. Gibbs. "I begin to think I shall never have the opportunity; my distinguished and most hospitable friend, Richard Tallant, Esq., has not yet honoured me with an invitation, even to a shooting-party, on the estate which calls him heir."

"Why, to tell you the truth," replied Mr. Tallant, junior, with an air of great candour; "I can't, you see; I've often thought I would make a clean breast of it, and tell you. The governor objects to you somehow or other; doesn't like you; wishes me not to ask you to Barton."

"That's candid, begad," said Mr. Gibbs, becoming a little redder in the face than usual. "Objects to me!"

"Stupid prejudice, but so it is; he doesn't understand bucks of fashion like you, Shuff; and he's heard about one or two of what you call your little affairs. And I am not very sorry either, Shuff; for I think the less he sees of you the better for me."

"You're devilish cool this morning, Dick Tallant, and—"

"And what?" said Mr. Tallant, hastily interrupting his friend, who showed unmistakable signs of anger. "Why, you know you're an infernal rascal, Shuff, and that I'm not much better myself; so let's have no brag about insults and all that sort of thing; I'm in with you for a short life and a merry one, so never mind the governor. *Il ne faut pas éveiller le chat qui dort*, as they say in France, vide Macdonnel."

Mr. Shuffleton exhibited his teeth, and haw-hawed several times, and Mr. Tallant, junior, slapped him on the back.

"You're a trump, Dick, 'pon my soul you are," said Mr. Shuffleton Gibbs, in an affected burst of magnanimity; "I was inclined to be savage just now, but I see the frankness of your disclosure in the true light, after your explanation."

"All right, old fellow," said Mr. Tallant, "give me your hand upon it, and we are Siamese twins again; but let us finish the sherry."

The two friends fell-to with a will after this, and chatted quite genially together about a hundred trivial things, until Big Ben tolled four o'clo k, when Mr. Richard Tallant mounted a splendid mare, and, followed by a sprightly groom on an animal of almost equal value, ambled towards the Park; whilst Mr. Shuffleton Gibbs betook himself quietly to his lodgings in Kensington Park Gardens, prior to keeping an engagement, he said, at the Corner, before dinner.

"The infernal impudent humbug," said Mr. Gibbs to himself, as he walked smartly homewards; "the twopenny-halfpenny mushroom, sprung from a northern dunghill—never mind, I'll be even with him some day. Fifty talents of silver invested in iron! Of late the fellow has assumed an air of superiority, and a bullying manner, which is devilish hard to bear. Wait a little, wait a little, *très bon ami;* you'll find yourself in the mire one of these days."

It *was* hard to bear, no doubt, but Richard Tallant was a very profitable investment to Mr. Shuffleton Gibbs, and he could afford to bottle up his Brummagem resentment; for such a fellow as Shuffleton Gibbs could hardly be said to have any honourable feelings of resentment. He was bankrupt, not only in purse, but in reputation; he might have got over the former in time, but he could never whitewash the latter.

Mr. Christopher Tallant had been proud of his son the first time he had seen him, prancing and capering in the Lady's Mile, as he pranced and capered soon after Mr. Gibbs left him. Mr. Tallant had gone down to the Park quietly on foot, and, unobserved, had seen his son a leading man of fashion, on the best horse amongst the most magnificent of all the splendid animals there. He had seen him acknowledged by many a dashing rider, and had watched him turn out into the carriage-drive, to ride beside a gorgeous yellow brougham, with beautiful women in it. Somehow the merchant could not help feeling annoyed with himself for harbouring such a pride as this; but he had not forgotten the Oxford epigram, and he liked to see a Tallant riding about amongst the big men, the greatest swell of the lot.

CHAPTER V.

THE DIBBLES AND THEIR NEW LODGER.

THOMAS DIBBLE, the porter, who held himself at the beck and call of the principals and officers of the Meter Iron Works Company at Westminster, lived in one of those numerous little streets which run off from the semi-aristocratic regions of St. George's Square, South Belgravia, to Whitehall; and his wife let lodgings and wore gorgeous caps.

She was quite a study this Mrs. Dibble, quite a psychological study. She governed Dibble, and yet made him her shield and protection in the most amusing and complete fashion. She was a fat, rubicund woman, with her dress either unfastened behind or before, and her cap hanging on the back of her head, both in summer and winter, as if she were in a perpetual state of perspiration.

She was by no means an ill-looking woman. Dibble in his cups had told his friends that she was a regular beauty when first he knew her, as fair as waxwork, sir. But her tongue; well it was a caution, Mrs. Dibble's tongue, and she had a sort of intermittent lisp, which instead of being an impediment in any way to the rapidity of her utterances only seemed to facilitate them, enabling her to slip and slide over an argument and abbreviate long words until her hearers might sometimes imagine she was pouring out a series of compound syllables in some unknown tongue. But that was only when she was in a passion, thank goodness, which did not occur more than once a week.

Dibble himself was a mild little fellow as a rule, and a profound admirer of Mrs. D.'s accomplishments. She had learnt to play the piano when she was at school in her youth; and when she sat down to a five-and-a-half octave square of Broadwood's on Sunday nights in her black satin·

dress, Dibble would sit by the fire and feast his eyes upon her with unsophisticated delight.

It was not a very symmetrical figure neither, Mrs. Dibble's, as you viewed it at the piano, and the two hooks and eyes which were undone near the middle of her back did not make it any the more elegant.

Mrs. Dibble usually thumped at the Old Hundredth and a wonderful variation of "Vital Spark," until her cap fell off and her hair came down, when she would close the "box of music" and utter twenty voluble regrets that she had so few opportunities of practising and keeping up her fingering.

But Mr. Dibble did not agree with her on this point; it was the only one he was permitted to dispute; he vowed she played as well as if she had no end of practice.

"You be fit for a concert," he would say, "that you be."

Not that Thomas Dibble exactly knew what a concert was, never having been present at anything of the kind, except on the occasion of a *soirée* at Gloucester when he went to a Sunday school there.

Dibble was bred and born in Gloucestershire, and had risen from a kitchen menial to a place in the household at Barton Hall two counties off, whither he had been recommended by a clergyman of the cathedral city. He was not in Mr. Tallant's service more than a year before he was promoted to the portership at West-minster.

The Barton housekeeper gave him an introduction to a relative of hers, Miss Wilhelmina Stikes, of Still Street, and after a few visits to that buxom spinster, Miss Stikes made love to Thomas, proposed to him, and married him in less than three months.

They had now been united some twenty years, and on the whole Mr. Dibble did not regret his bondage. He had always been accustomed to servitude; so the yoke of the fair-fat-and-loquacious Miss Stikes was not difficult to the patient and forbearing Thomas Dibble.

" So we are to 'ave a new lodger, Mithter Dibble, in the purthon of the bailifth's son ; well, so be it, though when my pa educated me for a lady, and being a builder he could do that because his property were naturally his own and if he had been thpared he would no doubt 'ave retired on it, educated for that thpere it never occurred to me that I should 'ave to take the hoffsprigs of bailifths into my house, but there is no knowing what we may come to, and if you fulfil the duties of the life which has come upon you, though without your own conthent I can't see after all that there's anything to be ashamed of," said Mrs. Dibble to her husband after a tripe supper, on the evening when Mr. Richard Tallant had promised to meet his friend Gibbs at the club.

"Yes, he be coming to-morrow; and I was thinking he might have the little back sittin' room," said Dibble, deferentially.

"Thank you, Dib, for your thoughts, but I may remark, as I have remarked before, that *I* will do the thinking; I did it for my pa during

all his contracts, and made out the thpethifica-
tions which were for two railway bridges, and
more than one or two streeth, and ith not un-
likely that I shall be fully competent to think for
you, Mithter Dibble; but, at the thame time, I
will own that I had thought of the back thitting-
room mythelf, and there's a chest of drawers bed
which Captain MacStrawsel, of the Blues, said
was a perfect bed of roses; and it may, therefore,
be fairly reckoned that a bailifth's son may recline
upon that which, if his conscience is at rest, he
may repose upon as well as in a palace."

Mr. Dibble said "Yes," and Mrs. Dibble mixed
for him, as was her wont, a mild glass of gin,
which he proceeded to sip in company with the
accomplished partner of his bosom, who in-
variably said, whenever she took spirits pub-
licly, "that it was not as she liked sperrits or
any other allycholic liquors, but it were a necessity to her, seeing the great strain that was
constant on her nerves, owing to having both
mental and physical labour more than common."

After a short visit to the farm, Paul Somerton went to London, and, after due introduction to Mrs. Dibble, entered upon his duties at the Iron Company's offices. He saw little of Mr. Richard Tallant, and less of his father; but he heard a great deal about both from old Dibble.

Once a week Mrs. Dibble permitted Thomas to spend an evening out with Paul. She said she was not one for letting a young man run about London in an evening without a guide, and she thought her Thomas's experience of the place might be of some benefit to Paul, and she would not hear of any opposition to an arrangement by which she proposed to set apart "closing time," on Friday nights until half-past ten, for Thomas Dibble to show Paul Somerton some of the sights of London.

Mrs. Dibble also at the same time arranged to entertain her own particular friends at home on these evenings, and so balanced off her generosity to poor Dibble, her husband. Thomas Dibble soon became a bore to Paul Somerton.

So soon as the young man began to know his way about town, so soon did he become tired of Dibble, and ashamed of him, too; for Paul was not altogether a stranger to the manners and feelings of a gentleman, and was a good-looking fellow withal; whilst poor Dibble was nothing more than a respectable porter at any time.

Besides, Dibble was perpetually praising Mrs. Dibble, and would stop to buy hot potatoes in the street, and "penn'orths" of pudding; so Paul decided to shake him off, but his determination was changed by a letter from his sister.

"What should Amy want to know all about Mr. Richard for?" said Paul, reading a letter in bed, one Sunday morning, some weeks after his residence in London.

"And who is Mr. Shuffleton Gibbs; and what the deuce business is it of hers if young Hammerton is often with them?" he continued, staring up from the letter to the ceiling.

"Please, sir, it's nine o'clock. Mrs. Dibble said

I were to tell you," said a voice through the keyhole.

"All right," said Paul ; " and hang Mrs. Dibble."

"Were I to say so, please ?" asked the voice.

"No, confound you," said Paul; " but tell Dibble I shall go for a walk with him after chapel."

It was the custom of Thomas Dibble to take what he called " a little constitutional " after chapel, and before dinner—just half-an-hour's stroll, whilst Mrs. Dibble changed her chapel-going satin, and dished up the dinner.

It was a rare thing for Mr. Paul Somerton to volunteer to accompany Mr. Dibble ; but he did so on the Sunday in question, and, as they walked by the Thames, watching the steamers pass and repass with their loads of noisy pleasure-seekers, Paul asked Dibble a variety of puzzling questions about Mr. Richard Tallant, and his friend, Shuffleton Gibbs.

"Ise no spy, Mr. Somerton, and Ise not an owl, or a dormouse," said Mr. Dibble, looking as knowing as he could at Paul.

"Certainly not, Dib," said Paul; "certainly not; you know a thing or two."

"Well, I dur say, and I knows nothing about the things you speaks of."

"What, don't you know who Mr. Gibbs is, and how he lives, and why he is a friend of the son's and not of the father's?" asked Paul.

"It bain't my business to know," said Mr. Dibble.

Paul Somerton pumped old Dibble all the way home, but to little or no purpose; and the porter's dogged silence aroused Paul's own curiosity about his sister's inquiries.

"Does Mr. Richard attend much at the office? Who and what is Mr. Gibbs? Are they particular friends of Mr. Hammerton? Do they meet together often? And where?"

These were the chief questions which Miss

Amy Somerton required her brother Paul to answer.

Paul was fond of his sister, and had always looked up to her as one of superior knowledge to himself.

"I'll tell you all you want to know, as soon as I can," he wrote to Amy on the Monday. "But why are you so inquisitive?"

There are thousands of brothers and sisters without affection for each other. We say of So-and-so, "I loved him as if he were my brother;" or, "Mary So-and-so—if she had been my own sister, I could not have felt more regard for her." It is flattering to our humanity that these illustrations of regard and affection should be in use. Nine families out of ten quarrel amongst themselves, and brothers and sisters are the deadliest enemies of brothers and sisters, thwarting each other in childhood and at maturity, stepping in each other's way, disgracing each other, and making the very name they mutually bear hateful to both. Happy, indeed, are brothers and sisters who really and truly love each other; for there is not a holier, not a more beautiful passion.

Paul Somerton would have done anything in the world for Amy. He remembered so many hours made happy by her love and foresight. They had nearly broken their hearts over parting when he went to school; and Amy had quite a box-full of his boyish letters, carefully preserved. She thought there was the making of a great man in Paul; he was like his father in temper and disposition—frank and outspoken, a hater of shams.

At first when Amy had written to him about the doings of Mr. Tallant, and concerning Mr. Hammerton, Paul had scruples about his duty in the matter; but it was sufficient for Paul that Amy assured him that she had a proper and sufficient object in learning what she sought; and Paul determined that Amy should soon know all she desired.

CHAPTER VI.

A FINE old Norman cathedral, by the side of a famous river—the one celebrated in history, the other a favourite with poets so long ago as Spenser.

The great grey cathedral, with its high pitched towers, and its crumbling walls, threw big dark shadows on the green turf of the college close, where half-a-dozen comfortable houses formed two sides of a square. In the centre grew a clump of venerable elms, the home of a colony of crows which were everlastingly calling to each other from above.

The other two sides of the square were filled in by the cathedral's grey walls, and an old gateway.

The river flowed on without—the famous river

with its sedgy banks. It flowed on outside the monastic-like square, noiselessly mostly, bearing lazy barges on its big brown bosom towards the sea. When the floods came down from the west it roared and whirled along in curls and eddies, the colour of coffee, like Kingsley's salmon river in the " Water Babies."

In the distance, from the upper windows of the cathedral close, on that side where Arthur lived, you could see the Linktown hills, with their graceful curving lines cut out against the sky; and if you had stood upon the Linktowns you might have seen another range of hills, which shut out Barton Hall from the rude world.

Arthur Phillips, as I have said, lived in this College Green, and his studio was at the top of one of those old houses, which had a glorious landscape before it, with the Linktowns for a background.

It was a curious old room, Arthur's studio, with mullioned windows in it, and a wonderfully carved fireplace, with. grinning heads cut in the mantelpiece. Several lay-figures were carelessly placed at one end of the room, and there were a couple of easels with half-finished pictures upon them. A few sketches in oil and in water-colours were hung about the room, and there was a guitar upon an old carved couch, and a large portfolio beside it. The artist wore a loose blouse, and looked at home in manner and appearance amongst his miscellaneous treasures.

Young Hammerton was a handsome fellow, one of a handsome stock. The Hammertons had been Earls of Verner for a century or more, and there was never known an ill-looking man or woman amongst them since the period when they came into the old island with the Norman Conqueror.

But there must have been much Saxon intermarrying in the family if one might judge from the fair skin and brown curly hair of Lionel Hammerton. And he was of sturdy make withal —a fine specimen of a handsome young Englishman, with a full hazel eye, and white regular teeth.

Lionel and Arthur had known each other for several years, the friendship commencing through a series of drawing lessons which Arthur Phillips had given Mr. Hammerton at Earl Verner's residence.

The Earl, Lionel's brother, was a man of great taste in the arts, and he had been Arthur's first patron.

Arthur had exhibited several pictures unsuccessfully at the great Midland Counties Exhibition, when Earl Verner singled out a landscape with figures in the foreground, by Mr. Phillips, as the best, the most conscientiously painted picture of that year.

This was Arthur's first start; the Earl purchased the picture, and the papers spoke of it in high terms of praise. The *Art Journal*, in a brief sketch of the Exhibition, noticed this painting as the work of one of the most promising artists of the day ; and next season two works of Arthur's were hung at the Royal Academy, and Success came unto him, and marked him for her own.

Earl Verner gave him several commissions, and placed Lionel Hammerton under him as a pupil, and this was how their friendship began.

He was a contrast to Arthur Phillips, who often noticed it, and drew little caricature sketches to illustrate it, which Lionel laughed at, and threatened to send to *Punch* as character studies.

Lionel had, indeed, once sent one of Arthur's funny bits to *Punch*, which brought a polite note from the editor of that famous periodical, soliciting a closer acquaintance with the artist; but Mr. Phillips was a lazy fellow, and his pencil only cut funny capers when Earl Verner's brother stirred him up, and suggested comical subjects.

"By Jove! if I were not to come in now and then, and laugh at you, you'd die of melancholy," said Lionel Hammerton, on one of his recent visits to Arthur's studio.

"No, I don't think that," said Arthur, lighting

the cigar which his friend handed to him; "but your society is fatal to dulness. I am too poor a companion to reciprocate the pleasure which your society gives me."

"Nay, dear boy, you are wrong there; I have spent some of my happiest hours in this old studio of yours, Arthur. What is it that makes an artist's den, as you call it, so free and easy, and yet so *distingué?*"

"One gets out of the world, and a little nearer the better land, in a room consecrated to art, even if the prophet be but a dotard, perhaps," said Arthur.

"And its perfect freedom—the absence of conventionality—the Bohemian character of the class called artists—their opposition to the forms and ceremonies, eh?"

"The artist only worships one goddess, I suppose; and she permits smoking, loose garments, unwashed hands, and slippers. Light your cigar," Arthur went on, carelessly, offering his friend a fusee.

"What a grand thing it is, too, the painter's art; of all arts the most delightful, the most satisfying! He is not like the writer, who must be read and studied before his audience can understand and enjoy what he has done. The effect of the artist's work on the beholder is instantaneous, the reward of his genius is immediate; to say nothing of his own personal delight and satisfaction. But I'm getting prosy, Arthur. Have you been into the Berne neighbourhood lately?"

"Yes, I was there during several days in last week," said Arthur.

"Well, any news, *mon ami:* are your friends all well?"

Arthur looked at Mr. Hammerton with a curious smile, as he replied, "Do not my views of Avonworth Valley give additional charms to my studio, Lionel?"

"News or views—which did you say? views, of course—well, so they do, and so they will continue to do, as long as you find such lovely bits of nature there," said Lionel, laughing

"Which do you prefer—the landscape or the figure studies?" Arthur inquired, still smiling, though a little sadly.

"I like them both; but there was a head which you were going to finish when I was here last. I don't see it anywhere," said Lionel, whose eyes had been wandering into every corner of the room.

"Here it is," said Arthur. "I have been making a double study of heads;" and he brought out of a small case, from a cupboard by the window, two water-colour sketches, and looked curiously into Lionel's face as his handsome friend examined them.

The first was something like that picture which appeared in the Strand shops some years afterwards.

Mr. Phillips had drawn the face full, and thrown the hair backwards in wavy folds. The lips were parted, and the eyes looked you in the face, full of hope and trust, and innocence.

Lionel laid this first study down, after a hasty glance or two at it, and then fairly " devoured " the second one.

A smothered sigh of relief escaped from Arthur as he noticed this, and a happy smile moved his lips as he watched the expression of approval which lit up Lionel's face whilst gazing at the darker beauty.

"By Jove," said Lionel, after a long pause, "it is exquisite! What a head! Talk of blood, why this head has all the character of a high-bred racehorse."

Arthur smiled, and puffed out a long thin wreath of smoke.

"What eyes! what a neck! And the hair bound tightly to the head, setting off those little ears! And the chin!—why, all the lines of beauty are exhausted here," Lionel went on; and Arthur almost trembled with delight.

"Give me your hand," he said at length, no longer able to control his feelings. "Give me your hand, Lionel Hammerton."

"With all my heart," said Lionel, looking as much astonished as he had previously been delighted. "But what, in the name of all the Arts and Sciences, is the matter with you? I'm not praising the painter, but the subject. You have not suddenly become vain, Arthur?"

"No, no," said the artist, pushing back his long black hair; "it is because you are praising the subject that I am delighted, Lionel. You love Amy Somerton."

"Stop, stop, not so fast, friend Arthur," said Lionel, colouring a little, and appearing still more surprised at the artist's unusual excitement.

"If you are in love at all, it is not with—with Miss Tallant?" Arthur went on, his big piercing eyes fixed intently on his friend.

"Oh, oh!" said Lionel, putting his hand upon Arthur's shoulder, and laying down Amy Somerton's portrait. "Oh, oh! Have I caught you in your own trap, my poor little friend?" said Lionel. "It is *you* who are in love! Nay, man, don't look so woe-begone about it."

"And you?" said Arthur, hanging his head like a schoolboy.

"May be some day, friend Arthur," said Lionel; "but *not* with Miss Tallant—*not* with Miss Tallant."

"Thank God for that!" said the artist, sitting down and fixing his eyes upon the distant hills, which the sun was making golden.

Lionel's manner of meeting Arthur's half confession of love for Miss Tallant and fear o rivalry, did not for the moment please the artist, whose sensitive nature revolted at the apparently cool and critical treatment of his friend.

But when young Hammerton said, "Arthur, my boy, don't fear me, go in and win," the artist forgot his momentary displeasure, and smiled half sadly, half comically, at his friend; and then told him how he had been unable to struggle against his admiration for Miss Tallant, and how it had ripened into love.

Lionel promising not to betray Arthur's confidence, laughed at the artist's notion that he was indulging in an utterly hopeless and futile passion.

"I suppose you will be at the Festival of the Three Choirs to-morrow," said Mr. Hammerton by-and-by, when they had changed the subject and he had lighted his last cigar.

"I shall be in some part of the building," Arthur said. "I have the *entrée* you know by certain private doors ; I am rather a favourite with the Dean and Chapter. I look down upon you from arches high up aloft, I listen to the music at various points. I should be too restless to sit all the time squeezed up amongst the audience."

Severntown, you must know, was celebrated for its Festival Concerts in the cathedral, which had been originated as early as 1724, resulting in noble collections for charitable purposes, and of which the local journalist a hundred years ago exclaimed, "May God grant that all charitable undertakings may be carried on with that becoming zeal and Ardency of Affection which

Matters of such allow'd Importance must always very justly claim !" Newspaper writers in those days, you see, said what they had to say briefly, and tersely, and to the point.

I mention these Severntown Festivals not with any intention of describing one of them, but simply because of the train of thought which the mention of the event by Mr. Hammerton excited in the mind of Arthur Phillips.

It was at the Festival, three years previously, that Arthur had first seen Phœbe Tallant, a mere girl, but of such striking beauty that the image was fixed in his mind, as if it belonged to the glorious music,—sanctified by the time, and the place, and the holy strains.

And he had gone on the following day, and peered out amongst the throng to see the same face again, but he saw it not; so he went quietly alone into the Lady Chapel to think of it, and build up the image in a picture of angels which he had thought, more than once, of painting. He never forgot the varied sensations which had been excited within him by that solitary ramble through private corridors into the Lady Chapel.

Shakspeare, Milton, and Pope have sung the delights of " hidden music." Who has not stood at night in some quiet churchyard with his thoughts reverentially turned to heaven by the solemn strains of an evening hymn rippling out through the half-open doorway? Who has not sat without the precincts of cathedral choirs and felt the power of religious strains move him more deeply than when in the presence of the choristers? Is it that the mind likes to fall back upon itself now and then, to wed the music to its own hopes and aspirations?

The Lady Chapel was quite shut out from the choir, nave, and aisles. As Arthur stood there the whole of the auditory and performers were completely away from view. The altar-screen was between him and the gay *parterre* of bonnets, hemmed in by the surrounding margin of baize and matting. Around him were decaying monuments, themselves needing memorials (as Crabbe puts it in "The Borough"); half-finished slabs fresh from the hands of the restorer, and other evidences of the struggle of the present to preserve the past.

Subdued morning beams came in through tiers of lancet lights; and mounting up, echoing along the fretted roof of the nave, the strains of the chorus came streaming in upon him over the screen, filling the little chapel with exquisite harmonies which seemed to die away in mysterious vaults and corridors. In pianissimo passages of solo or chorus the music receded, and died away in the west, like faint memories of former strains.

This was a memory worth cherishing; but it was fixed in the artist's mind as much by the association of the previous day as it was by its own intrinsic sublimity.

Six months afterwards it was that Arthur was introduced to Phœbe Tallant, and then that dear memory came back to him, softened into a kind of religious tint, as if it came through a painted window of the mind.

"This girl is my destiny," thought Arthur at once; for the face was always in his mind, and somehow it was mixed up with thoughts that were above the world, mixed up with dreamy pictures of cathedral aisles, and with memories of swelling anthems.

For a time, after he knew Phœbe, Arthur feared he was drifting into morbid sensibility. He had led a sober, monkish kind of life for years, and with this new image in his mind he had at first given himself up to wanderings about the old cathedral, and a sort of fascinating unreal saint-worship which he carried out for a time on canvas; but as time wore on he grew out of these morbid habits and once more there was a healthy glow in his conversation and in his pictures. But he was desperately, madly in love, nevertheless.

CHAPTER VII

IS A SENTIMENTAL CHAPTER, CONTAINING A FEW
MORAL REFLECTIONS BY THE WAY.

YES, Arthur Phillips was desperately in love.
A silly thing that, now-a-days, is it not? Love!
All very well in poetry and romance; all very
well for school-girls and beardless boys.

But may we not excuse an artist for fostering
such a ridiculous passion? It is something in his
line, you know. Painters, Senior Mammon will
probably say, are ridiculous fellows at best. They
spend their time in a fool's paradise, studying the
changes of the sky, making copies of trees and
leaves, and lashing themselves into furious excitement about the glories of summer mornings
and autumn sunsets.

You saw some of the race at Bettys-y-Coed, in

Wales, you know, Senior Mammon, when you were "doing" the neighbourhood of Snowdon. Poor devils! you remember how they were roaming about the rivers and rocks, and painting beneath umbrella tents. And you saw how some of them were content to live in those little cottages, and how they trudged about in the hot sun on foot, with their colour-boxes and things strapped to their backs.

Don't you remember saying to Signora Mammon that it was a pity the strapping fellows you meet at the Conway Falls are not better occupied than in sketching stones and trees.

You buy the artist's pictures sometimes, to keep him from starving, because you are charitably disposed,—eh, Senior Mammon? And to obtain for yourself a character for taste, as that sort of thing is necessary in polite circles,—eh, dear friend?

"But they are poor devils, after all," you say; and "an artist in love with Christopher Tallant's daughter must be an idiot indeed."

It is a pity Mr. Tallant is not informed of the tutor's infernal presumption, you say. He would soon send him to the right-about, he's such a proud fellow, you know, that Tallant.

"In love!" you repeat. "In rubbish! He should come with me, and air his little bit of brains on the Stock Exchange; he should know what it is to make a hundred thousand pounds in a week, and lose it in a day; he should see what women are, how they sell themselves body and soul for money."

There, friend Mammon, you need say no more. Arthur Phillips does not understand you, and if he did, he would continue in love with Miss Tallant just the same.

Strange, it must be to love a woman with all your heart and soul, and let her live on, unconscious of your admiration; to be with her, to listen to her sweet soft voice, to assist in the development of her taste, to minister to her fancy, to cultivate her love of the beautiful; and yet not dare to confess your love!

The river flowed on its way, and the sun went down behind the hills; the tones of the evening bell echoed through the college yard; and long after the heir of the Verners had left his friend, the artist sat smoking his cigar in the twilight, thinking of Phœbe Tallant—thinking of her as he might think of some beautiful vision of the poet—thinking of her with a love in his heart that was more than love. And yet she seemed a necessity in his life, something that made life worth living for—something next to his art.

He was quite alone in the world; he had neither mother nor father. He had been brought up in a quiet, humble way, and his father and mother both died before their son had achieved success as an artist.

It would have been the greatest happiness possible for him at that time, could he have shown his father the picture which first made his name known to the world as a painter. His mother had been a querulous invalid most of her life, and had few feelings in common with her son. The father, on the contrary, had been full of hope and trust in Arthur; but he was not to live to see these hopes realised.

So that Arthur's success had been tainted with a bitter sense of disappointment; he had no sympathiser in his triumph—none who knew how hard he had worked — none who knew the gigantic difficulties which he had overcome.

The people with whom he mixed knew him since success had come to his brush; and Phœbe Tallant had roused the strong feelings which had lain dormant within him.

His love, though excited by a sudden glimpse of the girl's beauty, had been strengthened by gradual growth, by little graceful acts, indications of sympathy and interest on the part of his pupil. He had struggled against it, and had felt once or twice that he was guilty of a breach of trust in harbouring such a passion for a moment.

It was true Mr. Tallant had asked him, as a favour, to give lessons to his daughter. The merchant, as you know, liked to have things which everybody could not have, no matter what he paid for them : and it was with something of this feeling that he had obtained the services of an artist who had suddenly risen above the necessity of teaching.

"I did not wish to come here at first," Arthur would argue to himself. "He almost forced me."

The idea of marrying Miss Tallant had never once occurred to Arthur. In the first place, he regarded his passion as a piece of presumption. He was unworthy in every respect, he thought, of Phœbe's love; and he never dreamed for a moment that she suspected the real state of his feelings towards her.

Although his name was so high in art, Mr. Tallant only looked upon Arthur as a tutor, and he would have regarded an offer of marriage for his daughter from such a source as an insult. But it was not in this mere worldly sense that Arthur felt himself inferior to Phœbe. His love and admiration had made a niche for her high up in his fancy, far beyond his brightest hopes, and he seemed to look up at her and worship, with a fearful, jealous, burning pleasure.

Who would have thought that so much passion could have a place behind that calm, thoughtful, and reserved manner of the landscape painter?

CHAPTER VIII.

IN WHICH PAUL SOMERTON ENTERS UPON A
DELICATE, DIFFICULT, AND DANGEROUS TASK.

MR. RICHARD TALLANT was a member of several
London clubs. The one to which his friend Mr.
Shuffleton Gibbs invited him was a third-rate
establishment, rapidly degenerating into a mere
association of gamblers.

The members met in an evening and kept up
in appearance mild whist at shilling points; but
large bets were made upon the odd tricks, " each
and every."

Loo was not permitted because it was too much
of a gambling game. The Ashford Club assumed
a virtue they did not possess. Members might
bet a thousand pounds on the odd trick at whist,
but they must not play Loo.

It was here that Mr. Shuffleton Gibbs made most of his money, and there was every reason to fear that Richard Tallant was not above helping him. The spirit of gambling had fairly taken possession of Richard's mind, and he sank with it into the practice of all sorts of vices.

In the City Mr. Richard Tallant was known as a young, wealthy, devil-may-care fellow, a man to know, and a man to fear. He often speculated largely, unknown to his father, and had more than once "rigged" the share market to great advantage. His position gave him excellent opportunities to obtain information which was of financial value, and Shuffleton Gibbs was deep enough to put his friend up to all sorts of stock-jobbing tricks that often turned him in good round sums of money.

One would have thought that this legalised gambling would have been sufficient for Mr. Tallant and his friend Gibbs; but Gibbs was an old card-sharper; he loved the fierce excitement of the table, and there was more certain success in a doctored card and a loaded dice than in stock-jobbing.

You see we don't at all disguise Mr. Gibbs's character; he was a thorough-paced blackguard, and Mr. Richard Tallant was graduating very successfully in the Blackguard school. At present he is not aware that Gibbs is indebted to anything but skill for his success at cards: he has never seen the disgraced Oxford *roué's* private room.

Paul Somerton's inquiries had not led him to a knowledge of all that we have here set down; but in less than a month he had come to the conclusion that Mr. Shuffleton Gibbs was a scoundrel, and that Mr. Richard Tallant was not conducting himself in a manner calculated to uphold the honour of his father's name.

And young Hammerton, the heir to the earldom of Verner: no good could come of his association with Mr. Gibbs and Tallant junior. How persistent Amy was in her inquiries about Mr. Hammerton!

"I can't see why you be so anxious to know all

about their goings on," said Mr. Thomas Dibble, in one of their once-a-week perambulations.

"Well, never mind, old boy," said Paul; "you and I are good friends and always will be. Why cannot we have our little confidences like other people ? "

" No reason at all," said Dibble, looking round at a baked-potato stove.

"Have a potato ?" said Paul, stopping his friend forcibly as they were turning into Piccadilly.

Mr. Dibble stared at him to see if he were in earnest.

"All right, old boy; I know you like them; have one, don't mind me."

Dibble instantly complied with Paul's request, and was soon engaged in devouring the mealy esculent.

In a few minutes he said, as well as he could speak with a mouthful of the baked tempta-tion,—

"That be kind of you now, Master Paul, very ; you knows I likes taters,—we've all our likes and

dislikes, eh, Mister Somerton ? My weakness is
Mrs. Dibble and baked pertaters !"

"And pudding, old Dib—now confess."

Old Dibble laughed, and said Paul was a regular
good un ; and from this the porter was easily led
on to repeat little things which he occasionally
saw and heard in Mr. Richard Tallant's room.

Whilst they were talking, a brougham pulled up
to the edge of the pavement, and Paul saw that
it was occupied by the Hon. Lionel Hammerton.

"Let us wait here a few moments, Dib; I think
I know that gentleman," said Paul, detaining his
friend.

A smart footman leaped from the box,
opened the carriage door, and out stepped Mr.
Hammerton, who immediately disappeared up a
flight of steps which led into a dingy but rather
ostentatious building.

"Dib, old boy, we must see what place this
is."

"This ?" said Dibble; "why it be the Ashford
Club. I know Mister Fencer, who takes care of

the rooms; Mrs. Fencer be quite a crony of Mrs. Dibble's."

"The Ashford Club, eh ? I should like to have a peep at the place inside, Dib."

"Well, that be easy enough, I s'pose. Let us call and ask Mr. Fencer how he be."

They went up the flight of stone steps, and found Mr. Fencer, who patronised Mr. Dibble in majestic style.

Fencer was a fussy, pompous person, as was also Mrs. Fencer, who was absent this evening; being, in fact, on a visit to Mrs. Dibble. Fencer, therefore, was fussier and more pompous than usual, and he took Mr. Somerton and Dibble into his little room and treated them to hot gin-and-water, *ad libitum.*

By-and-by Paul Somerton insiduously got on the blind side of Mr. Fencer, and obtained permission to go and have a peep into the card-room; where Paul, through a half-opened door, saw Mr. Richard Tallant, Mr. Shuffleton Gibbs, Mr. Hammerton, and another gentleman, seriously occupied at cards. There were several other little card parties in the room, but Paul had no eyes for any other table than that at which the Hon. Lionel Hammerton was seated. Earl Verner's brother was evidently the greatest loser, though his partner, Mr. Tallant, was also betting heavily, and unsuccessfully it seemed, with the fourth gentleman, who was unknown to Paul.

This was enough for the present. Paul joined Fencer and Dibble again, making himself particularly agreeable to the former, and promising to pay him another visit on the first opportunity that occurred.

Meanwhile Paul cared for nothing more but to get back to Pimlico and to bed. There was something wrong going on, Paul was sure ; he would write to Amy in the morning and reply fully to her inquiries.

Dibble was particularly communicative on the way home, on account of Fencer's large dose of gin ; he told Paul that he would stick to him till death, and tell him anything he knew. He believed Mister Gibbs was no better than a swindler, and his master's son was surely a reprobate.

"You should have heard what Fencer told me private," Dibble went on, nodding his head, and clinging hard and fast to Paul Somerton's arm : "that Mister Gentleman Gibbs is a sort of Jeremy Diddler, sir, depend on it; and master's son is, they do say, the fastest man about town."

"Indeed! all right, Dib. I'll hold you up, old boy," said Paul, as Dibble plunged and fought his way through an imaginary crowd of obstructions.

Dibble gradually becoming helpless, Paul was compelled to call a cab; and they reached Still Street just in time to find Mrs. Dibble alone and in good humour.

But a change rapidly came over the salubrious calm when Mrs. Dibble noticed Thomas's neck-tie twisted round to the back of his neck, and saw him gazing at her in a helpless state of idiotic admiration and amazement.

Turning upon Paul she poured out such a volley of declamation against deceit, and the lead-

ing of innocence into temptation and sin, that Paul
was fain to rush off to bed, and leave poor Dibble
to contend with the remainder of the storm. He
heard the matrimonial tempest raging for fully
an hour after he had retired, until at length it
gradually subsided, and peace was proclaimed in
the sonorous snore of Dibblonian repose.

It was long past midnight when the last card-
party at the Ashford Club broke up. Young
Hammerton and Richard Tallant left together,
and Hammerton accepted the offer of a bed at
Mr. Tallant's house in Connaught Place, where a
cab soon deposited them.

The moon shone peacefully over the park as
they crossed it, and made silvery sparkles on the
windows of the long, fashionable row of houses.

The trees stood out in the uncertain lights,
with early spring leaves upon them. The long
rows of lamps looked yellow and out of place in
the pure light of the moon; and the distant
whistle of a railway engine seemed all the more
to mark the morning stillness.

That whistle came home to Lionel Hammerton; it seemed to upbraid him, and at the same time invite him to the country of the Berne Hills. He had promised to return to his brother (who had been lying ill there for several weeks) two days ago; but the infatuation of play had come upon him, and his large losses of this evening had prompted him to endeavour to retrieve his ill-luck on the morrow. Mr. Gibbs had promised him his revenge, and Tallant and he were pledged to visit the Ashford on the next night.

Mr. Tallant was light-hearted enough over his losses, whilst Hammerton sat gloomily thinking of his, and the sick brother, for whom he had a real affection. Mr. Richard Tallant hummed bits of an operatic chorus, and the most popular bars of the latest waltz.

The two card acquaintances said scarcely a word until they bade each other good night; and before Mr. Tallant was up the next day the Hon. Lionel Hammerton was steaming away on the

Great Western to the halls of his fathers by the
Berne Hills.

A glorious old place that castle where Earl
Verner resided, full of odd nooks and corners,
with quaint gables, and grey, ivy-clad turrets ; a
castle which had held out for months during the
great rebellion.   The older portion had been sup-
plemented with some new buildings designed in
harmony with the ancient architecture of the
original building.

Before this history is complete the reader may
be called upon to visit Montem Castle : until
then it is not necessary, perhaps, to say more
than that it was the ancient seat of the Verner
family.

CHAPTER IX.

IT was pleasantly situated at the top of Berne
Hills. It had originally been a watch-tower, but
Mr. Tallant had converted it into what they
called the summer-house. There were comfortable seats in it, and a few odd books and pictures.
It commanded sixty miles or more of scenery,
flat, undulating, and mountainous ; wood, water,
and pastures ; towns, villages, and hamlets.

You might search the country through, and
not find a scene more truly English and more
perfectly beautiful. In spring, if you journeyed to that summit from Barton Hall,

when the sun was shining and the sky serene, you might fancy yourself in the Happy Valley indeed.

The way is over meadows, down lanes, up sloping hill-sides, through woods, and by rippling water-courses. There are violets in the hedge-rows, and daffodils in the meadows, and primroses in the woods. Anemones tremble in secluded thickets, and there are fruit-trees in bloom in the distant orchards, that gleam through the faintly green trees.

Phœbe Tallant and Amy Somerton walked up to the summer-house several times in the spring and summer months; sometimes they rode part of the way on rough ponies, but oftener they walked the whole distance, interrupted only by a stray deer from the adjacent park of Montem Castle or a fox from the Berne covers. Only, did I say, by a deer or a fox? Truly; for was not Mr. Phillips a fox, to sketch so continually amongst those Berne Hills?

The day after Amy Somerton had received her

brother's full report about Mr. Hammerton, she proposed a walk to the summer-house, and Miss Tallant gladly accepted the challenge.

Phœbe was always ready for a long ramble; and the spring sunshine on this day was particularly inviting.

Taking their alpine sticks and donning their jauntiest hats, our two fair maidens, arm in arm, passed over the smooth, green lawn, and soon disappeared behind the shrubs and trees.

Luke Somerton, who had been up into the woods for a brace of rabbits, watched them unobserved as they entered the lane near Barton Hall, and an expression of pride lighted up his manly face as he gazed on the supple and graceful form of his daughter Amy.

Richard Tallant spoke truly when he was joking Mr. Shuffleton Gibbs about Somerton's beautiful daughter. It would have been as much as any man's life were worth to have insulted Amy Somerton in the knowledge of her father.

" I tell you, Luke Somerton," said Mrs. S.,

when Luke entered the house, "that Mr. Hammerton is bent upon no good with regard to Amy."

" Stuff and nonsense ! " said Luke, laying down his rabbits, and putting his gun into a case by the fireplace.

" When you see a fox about the fold-yard, what do you think he is seeking ? " asked Mrs. Somerton, sneeringly.

" Foxes be hanged ! " said Luke.

" And fools be hanged ! " said Mrs. Somerton, banging the door, and leaving her liege lord to his own thoughts.

" By all means," said Luke, still thinking of the handsome women whom he had seen in the lane.

" And that painter fellow," said Mrs. Somerton, returning ; " he's in the woods yonder. Old Tallant must have lost the small portion of brains that God gave him to begin with, if he can't see that his daughter is befooling him."

" Why, Sarah, you are mad on this point. These girls seem to worry your life out."

" Mad ? You may trust a mother's eyes, Luke Somerton, to see what's going on. I tell you, that ugly little blackamoor painter-fellow is making love to Miss Tallant, and that the future Lord Verner is sneaking about after our Amy."

" The future Lord Verner after Amy !—stuff ! you're dreaming, wife," said Luke.

" Some people's dreams are as good as the waking thoughts of other people," Mrs. Somerton replied.

" Well, we shall see—we shall see," said Luke, carelessly.

" Yes, when it's too late," Mrs. Somerton rejoined, with an emphatic nod of her head.

And so the subject dropped. Meanwhile Phœbe and Amy were enjoying the spring sunshine at the top of Berne Hills. The glorious beams shot down upon the landscape from behind little scudding clouds, and made the beech-trees shine like silver.

The river that wound its way from east to west shone out here and there in great white patches.

·Hundreds of shifting shadows fell upon hill and dale ; lulling sounds came up the hills from the villages round about ; the birds sung as they only sing in Avonworth Valley ; and everything breathed of peace, content, and happiness.

"And so you think Mr. Hammerton is getting into bad company, Amy?" said Miss Tallant, when the two fair girls had sat down to rest in the summer-house.

"He is, indeed," said Amy, seriously.

"Gambling ?"

"Yes ; to a dreadful extent, Paul says."

"May I see the letter, dear?" Miss Tallant asked, laying her hand affectionately on Amy's shoulder.

"I tell you candidly, Phœbe dear, I do not like to let you see what Paul says about your brother."

"Don't mind that. I have long since believed my brother to be much less noble in his conduct than could be desired," said Phœbe.

"Have you ever heard of his friend, Mr. Gibbs ?"

" No, dear. Who is he ? "

" Oh, a dreadful man, I believe ; unfit altogether for the society of your brother."

" Indeed," said Mr. Richard Tallant, in a
whisper, as he stood quietly smoking a cigar near
the open doorway of the summer-house. " The
conversation becomes interesting."

" In what respect ? " asked Phœbe.

" Why, dear, Paul has made every possible
inquiry, and he pronounces him to be no better
than a swindler; and he says many men have been
transported and hanged who have done nothing
worse than Mr. Gibbs has done," said Amy,
with animation.

" Those are strong words, Amy," said Miss
Tallant.

" They are, by Jove ! " said her brother
to himself; " but true, I believe, by my
soul ! "

" Not too strong, I fear, Miss Tallant," Amy
went on ; "and——but I would rather not show
you the letter."

" Now you are getting angry, *Miss* Somerton," said Amy, kissing her companion's cheek.

" Forgive me, dear Phœbe ; I did not mean to use that odious word, ' Miss.' "

And then the two girls kissed each other, and Amy handed Paul's letter to Miss Tallant without more ado.

" By Jove ! " said Richard Tallant to himself, " that sister of mine is a perfect fool. The bailiff's daughter is fairly master of her ; and, egad, I don't wonder at it."

" This is indeed dreadful. Your brother has certainly been indefatigable. Richard the associate of gamblers and the loosest men in town, and sanctioning a plot to ruin Mr. Hammerton ! This truly is sad news," said Miss Tallant, reading Paul's letter, and commenting upon it as she read.

" Yes, by Jove ! " said Mr. Richard Tallant, dropping the remains of his cigar, and crushing it under his heel. " So-ho, Master Sneak ! I'll be even with you, my fine fellow. A devilish nice thing to be tracked about by a junior clerk, set on by his sister, the daughter of my father's bailiff. We'll see about this. Shall I play the eaves-dropper any longer?"

" And what have you said in reply?" Phœbe asked, folding the letter, and returning it to Amy.

" I have told Paul he must warn Mr. Hammerton in some way; that he must take means to let him know that he is being duped."

" You are putting too much on the boy's shoulders, I think," said Phœbe.

" Oh! I wish I were a man for one month—just for a month, Phœbe," said Miss Somerton, starting from her seat, her eyes sparkling, and her little mouth pursed up. " But, alas! I am only a woman, and a vain, weak, silly creature, I fear," she continued, re-seating herself and sighing.

" Weak and silly!" said Phœbe, quietly. " Why weak and silly?" Then dropping her voice and putting her arm round Amy's waist, she asked: " Do I know why you call yourself weak and silly?"

Amy started and blushed, and bent her head, spirited and full of mettle as she appeared to be a moment previously.

"Don't blush, Amy dear. Do I know why you blush?" and Phœbe kissed her companion's forehead.

"I am a vain, silly, stupid creature, Phœbe; and you must despise me."

Phœbe only pressed her friend's hand in reply.

"You must easily have read all my heart to-day," Amy went on, trembling at her own temerity. "Paul's letter, my hasty words this morning, my interest in his doings, my——"

"Of course, of course," said Phœbe, quite in a reassuring, comforting way: "you love Mr. Hammerton. There, don't start, my dearest, like that. I *know* you do, and why should you not?"

Pale and trembling Amy looked for a moment at her friend, and the tears started into her eyes.

"You must think me mad," she said.

"Indeed I do not, my pet," said Phœbe, quite cheerfully, and kissing Amy again. "It is natural to love a fine, dashing fellow like Mr. Hammerton; quite natural in a high-spirited girl like you."

"It is madness, vanity, and everything that is weak," said Amy.

"Nonsense, nonsense, child!" Phœbe replied. "You are worthy the love of the finest gentleman in England."

"Ah, Phœbe! you and I know but little of the world. Mr. Hammerton is as far above me as a prince is above a peasant. I am foolish, wickedly foolish, to have permitted my liking to have got the better of my judgment."

"Why, I could almost venture to say Mr. Hammerton is in love with you as much as you are in love with him," said Phœbe, cheerily.

Amy shook her head sadly, as she thought of the difference between them in rank and station.

"Bless me!" said Phœbe, divining her thoughts; "princes have married peasant-girls before now, and shall not an earl's son—and only a younger son, remember—be proud of the love of a true and noble heart like yours ? "

Phœbe grew quite eloquent and enthusiastic. " Consult your favourite poet when we return, Amy, and read about King Cophetua."

" I need not ask you never to breathe a word of my silly confession to anyone at any time ? " said Amy, now a little more like her former self.

" Trust me," said Phœbe, as she gathered up her hat and cloak, which had lain upon the table.

" My feelings overcame me; but it is a relief now, even to have confided my weakness and vanity to you," said Amy; and then the two impulsive beauties embraced each other again.

" Humph ! " said Mr. Richard Tallant, " I must have a hand in this pretty little business."

CHAPTER X.

"AHEM! pleasant occupation truly," said Mr.
Richard Tallant, planting himself in the centre of
the summer-house doorway, and contemplating
the ladies, who stared in astonishment at the
apparition.

"Any objection to take me into your em-
braces?" he went on, smiling, walking up to
Miss Tallant, kissing her on the forehead, and
bowing very politely to her companion.

"Why, how long have you been standing
there, Richard?" asked Miss Tallant, in some
confusion.

"Not long," said Richard, fixing his eyes on
Miss Somerton; "but long enough to be delighted

at the charming picture of affection which you presented to the view."

"You have brought your town compliments with you, Richard," said Phœbe. "I fear they will be wasted upon us poor provincials."

"I hope not; as I have come down to spend a couple of days with you," said Richard.

Miss Somerton said nothing, but she was convinced, by Mr. Tallant's manner, that he had heard at least a portion of her conversation with his sister.

"I am sorry I interrupted your *tête-à-tête*," said Mr. Tallant. "I fear my sudden presence has not pleased Miss Somerton. You see, I wanted a little rest and quiet, and hearing that Mr. Hammerton was at home I thought I would first run down, spend a couple of days with you and the governor, and then ride over to Montem and see a certain noble swell, who has a little business with me. When I got to the house, I found nobody in; so I followed you up here and smoked my cigar. I have enjoyed the walk, I assure you; 'pon my honour, I have not had such a treat for a long time."

Mr. Tallant and Amy Somerton eyed each other more than once during this little speech, and Amy was more and more convinced that Richard Tallant had played the listener, which made her for a time constrained in her manner; by-and-by she threw over her anxiety a forced liveliness, which did not escape the notice of Mr. Tallant.

"Shall I have the honour of escorting you to Barton Hall?" he said; for by this time the ladies had left the summer-house.

"We shall be honoured by so much condescension," said Phœbe, smiling archly. "Shall we not, Amy?"

"Very much so indeed," said Miss Somerton; "and perhaps Mr. Tallant will entertain us with the latest fashionable news."

"By all means," said Richard. "Lady Cooling has run away with her groom; Viscount Fusswell has married the *piquante* Miss Morris,—she was a governess, I think, or something of the sort, and she's a deuced jolly girl. Do you care about scandal, Miss Somerton, by the way, or will you have another sort of gossip ? "

"Ask Miss Tallant, sir," said Amy. "I have no right of choice in this matter."

"Then I don't like it," said Phœbe. "What is that little poem I was reading the other day somewhere ?" she said stopping, and tapping her foot with her climbing-staff.

"Ah, what is it, Phœbe ?

> ' Phœbe, dearest,
>   Tell, oh tell me,' "

said Richard, humming one of the English tenor's favourite ballads.

> " ' A whisper broke the air,"—

said Phœbe, pausing. "Now I remember :—

> ' A whisper broke the air,--
>   A soft light tone, and low,
>   Yet barb'd with shame and woe ;
> Now, might it only perish there,
>   Nor further go !

Ah me! a quick and eager ear
  Caught up the little meaning sound!
Another voice has breathed it clear,
  And so it wander'd round
From ear to lip, from lip to ear,
Until it reach'd a gentle heart,
  And that—*it broke.*"

"Bravo, sis! bravo Phœbe!—delivered with fine effect," said Mr. Tallant. "May I smoke one cigar, just one?"

"With pleasure," said Phœbe. "What do you say, Amy dear?"

"I have not the smallest objection; I rather like it."

"It is better than scandal, infinitely,—eh, Miss Somerton?" said Mr. Tallant, lighting a Cabana.

"Much," said Amy.

"What do you think now," said Richard, "they have been saying about me?"

"I seldom go to London," said Amy.

"Why, a fellow told me that some scandal-monger or other was setting it about that I am very fast, that I gamble."

"Oh! that is dreadful," said Miss Somerton, quickly. "That you are a gambler?"

"Yes—fact, 'pon my life," said Richard.

"They could not say anything worse about you than that, Mr. Tallant. A gambler, I think, is the most despicable creature."

"Of course," said Richard, looking at Miss Somerton with a curious expression of face.

"Since we have had one quotation, perhaps you will pardon another that has direct reference to this point—a line from Talfourd. I have been reading about gaming lately."

Miss Somerton looked earnestly at Mr. Tallant, for now she was sure he had heard what she had said in the summer-house.

"Indeed! Pray enlighten us," said Mr. Tallant.

"Gaming, sir, for its own sake, will destroy the noblest nature, and ruin the wealthiest.

'What meaner vice
Crawls there than that which no affections urge,
And no delights refine?'

It

> ' Changes enterprise
> To squalid greediness, makes heaven-born hope
> A shivering fever, and in vile collapse
> Leaves the exhausted heart without one fibre
> Impell'd by generous passion.' "

"Really, 'pon my honour—why, you two fair ladies must have been studying elocution and all that sort of thing lately," said Richard, flicking off the top of a young ash-plant with his cane.

"I'm glad you condemn those scandalous aspersions of my character, Miss Somerton; though, you see, all that pretty poetry is not much good, for everybody gambles one way or another in turn You should see the big guns who do it in the City—real out-and-outers—members of Parliament, and swells of the first water—I mean in buying and selling shares, and what they call rigging the market, and all that sort of thing. Why, the governor himself has done a little in that way in his time. But let me see, where were we? Oh, about what people say. Well, I was told the other day that young Hammerton was fond of cards; but, bless us, there is always lots of scandalous things said about young fellows of position; indeed, I heard something of Hammerton the other day which is hardly proper to mention before ladies, and yet he's as good a fellow as there is going—don't you think so, Miss Somerton?"

"That I certainly do," said Amy, fully prepared for the sly attack; "but many a good man has been led astray by ill-chosen companionship."

"'My son, if sinners tempt thee,' &c.,—I see, yes," said Richard, with a slight sneer.

"You may laugh, Mr. Tallant," said Amy, blushing at her own temerity; "but many a free, generous-minded man has been brought to misery by the companionship of a bad man, professing friendship which he never felt or understood."

"That reminds me," said Mr. Tallant; "the same fellow who told me that he had heard I gambled, told me that hard things were said of another man whom I meet sometimes. Of course

I cannot be answerable for the character of every fellow I meet; it is all envy, hatred, and malice."

" Bad company," said Amy, " is like a nail driven into a post, which after the first and second blow may be drawn out with little difficulty; but being once driven up to the head, the pincers cannot take hold to draw it out, but which can only be done by the destruction of the wood. We had to turn that sentence into hexameters the other day by order of Signor De Maury, our linguistic master," said Amy; " I think it rather a fine simile."

" Indeed ? yes, perhaps it is," said Mr. Richard Tallant, thinking to himself that the girl was " infernally impudent."

By this time they had reached the last coppice, prior to coming out into the open before Barton Hall; and at a picturesque bend in the somewhat intricate footpath, they came suddenly upon Mr. Phillips, the artist, who was sitting quietly contemplating a half-sketched-in clump of spring foliage, pierced with a broad ray of sunlight.

The artist's long black hair was thrown back, his hat lying on the ground, and his sharply-cut features were lit up with a smile of satisfaction.

He had worked at this little sketch for many days, and had only just accomplished what he considered to be a reasonable approach to the production of a peculiar effect of sunlight upon firs and larches and silver beech, with a background of rock and sky, in early spring.

For a moment he sat unconscious of the audience which stood before him—one a lady, who had to make an effort to hide her agitation.

"Hope you're satisfied, old boy," said Mr. Tallant, approaching the artist.

"Good morning—good morning, ladies," said Mr. Phillips in his deep mellow voice, and advancing to meet the party.

"Ah! deuced good—capital," said Richard, standing in front of the easel.

"Do you think so?" said the artist. "What do you think, Miss Tallant? I have been work-

ing at this poor trifle of study, I am ashamed to
say how long."

"I am sure you need not be ashamed," said
Miss Tallant, quietly.

"You have been highly successful, as you
always are," said Miss Somerton.

"Come along, Phillips, come along; we are
going to have luncheon. The governor is away,
and I'm master to-day. Come along, and we'll
talk about the world and what it says. You
ought to have been up the hill with us; my lady
friends have been wonderfully eloquent about
good boys and naughty boys, and all sorts of
things. Tommy was a good boy; he said his
lessons, and never went into bad company, and he
got some nice cake. Billy was a bad boy, and he
wouldn't say his lessons, and he was whipped, and
he got no cake. There, don't be angry, Miss
Somerton," said Richard, rattling on and laughing
at Amy, evidently glorying in what he had heard;
and yet piqued at her covert replies to his pre-
tended gossip.

"Angry! not I, Mr. Tallant.   If Tommy is good, Tommy will be rewarded, at any rate, with an approving conscience ; and Billy—why, if he is bad, he will assuredly be punished.   And so let us go to luncheon."

"Hear, hear !   Come along, Phillips ;" and as soon as the artist was ready they all went together over the lawn, and disappeared within the handsome portals of Mr. Tallant's princely residence.

CHAPTER XI.

THE drawing-room, library, and dining-room at Barton Hall were upon the ground-floor, *en suite.* They had their several and separate entrances from the hall and corridor beyond; and at the same time had communications with each other from within.

The library was the centre apartment, with the dining and drawing-room on either hand; so that, two doors being open, you could walk in a direct line from one end of the suite of rooms to the other ; and a delightful walk it was, lit up by seven or eight magnificent bay-windows, from each of which there were glorious views of the Berne Hills.

The little party which entered the house at the close of our last chapter, having lunched, adjourned into the library, where the window opening from the ground was thrown up, in order that Mr. Richard Tallant might sit just within and smoke one more cigar.

Miss Somerton strolled into the next room, and sat down to the piano, letting her fingers wander dreamily over the keys.

Where he sat Mr. Tallant had, through the open doorway, a side-view of her beautiful head; and feelings of disappointment, jealousy, admiration, and annoyance, successively took possession of him as he smoked, and looked, and listened.

Mr. Phillips was absorbed in the examination of some new illustrated books which Mr. Christopher Tallant had sent from town for Phœbe, who must have the artist's opinion about them.

The artist talked about high art, ideality, and poetic licence. He thought certain Dante pictures too literal in their interpretation of the horrors of the "Inferno," and he called some of the sketches morbid and sensational. He was in raptures with half-a-dozen pictures in a work of fairy fiction; but he was thinking all the while a great deal more of Phœbe's beauty than of anything else.

Mr. Richard Tallant could not help noticing the remarkable contrast between the artist and his sister as they stood together looking at the new books.

The fair *spirituelle* face of the woman set in that sunny halo of soft brown hair; and the sharp and highly intellectual features of the artist intensified by the long black hair which fell upon the somewhat rounded shoulders.

It brought to his mind for a moment a famous pre-Raphaelite picture ; but his thoughts wandered away instantly to Amy Somerton, who was softly touching out the melody of " Life let us Cherish," from amongst a wealth of unobtrusive variations which Arabella Goddard has since made so pleasantly familiar.

" And she loves young Hammerton, does she?"

he thought, whilst he smoked and nursed his
left leg, and occasionally stroked his full black
moustache. "Love's the probable successor to an
earldom. She aims high. Well, so be it. The
fellow's good-looking and conceited: he'll humour
the lady's fancy, of course. He can't marry her;
that's out of the question. She evidently thinks
I'm a blackguard—that's not so pleasant; but
Master Paul shall pay for that."

The next moment the Hon. Lionel Hammerton
was announced, whereupon Miss Somerton rose
from the piano, and the new comer was shown
into the library.

"Who would have thought of seeing you?"
said Mr. Tallant, throwing his cigar at a blackbird (which was hopping about on the lawn),
and coming forward to greet Mr. Hammerton,
who was receiving a cordial welcome from Miss
Tallant.

"How do you do?" said the young aristocrat,
extending his hand. "Phillips, my friend, and
how are you? I'm delighted to see you."

"The delight is mutual," said Arthur, shaking Mr. Hammerton heartily by the hand.

"I saw one of your last pictures at Earl Stanton's place in town three days ago," said Mr. Hammerton, "with three wonderful connoisseurs going frantic about it. The Earl had given a hundred and fifty guineas for it, they said. What do you think it was, Miss Tallant?"

"A landscape?" said Phœbe, with an inquiring smile.

"Well, I suppose it might be called a landscape. It was a bit of the lake yonder, in the corner of the park, with a clump of trees at the back, and some ducks amongst the grass and reeds at the side of the pool—nothing more—a mere sketch, which Mr. Phillips can rub in, as he calls it, in little more than a week. Your trees and hedges, and cows and poultry, and bits of lake and brook, and rock and hill, at Barton here, are a fortune to Mr. Phillips."

The artist smiled and shook his head.

"Why, you Crœsus, you know it is true," said

Mr. Hammerton. " He will soon be as rich as my dear brother is reputed to be, Miss Tallant ; he literally coins money does my friend Arthur ; but what is better—and if he were not here, I should be tempted to say more—he paints for the love of his art, and he is as noble a fellow as ever sat before an easel. There ! "

The young nobleman seemed bent upon exalting the moral and pecuniary worth of Mr. Phillips. He might have had an object to serve in placing his friend's merits and advantages before Mr. Tallant and his sister, and he laid particular emphasis on " my friend Phillips," or " my friend Arthur," and spoke of him with the familiarity of pure regard and esteem.

" By-the-by," said Mr. Hammerton after a pause, " let me explain my unexpected visit to Mr. Tallant. Don't go away, I beg, Miss Tallant."

" I will return again before you leave, thank you," said the lady in her sweetest accents.

" I heard you were here, sir," said Mr. Hammerton, resuming an aristocratic dignity of manner, which he assumed with those who were not his intimates (he had not met Mr. Tallant junior frequently), "and thinking you might deem it necessary to give me a call, I preferred to anticipate you."

Mr. Tallant bowed, and twirled his moustache carelessly.

"Allow me to present you with a little token of our last meeting," Mr. Hammerton continued, handing Mr. Tallant a sealed envelope.

"Thanks ; you are very good," said the Iron Prince, dropping the note into the side pocket of his loose morning coat.

"Will you not look at it, and see that it is quite right ?"

"No, thank you; I have no fear about that. Shall I offer you a cigar ? The ladies will allow us to smoke on the lawn just outside the window."

Mr. Tallant handed Mr. Hammerton his cigar-case.

"May I offer one to my friend ?" said Mr.

Hammerton, looking round for Mr. Phillips, who had strolled into the drawing-room.

"By all means. Mr. Phillips, will you do me the pleasure of joining us in a cigar?" said Mr. Tallant, raising his voice; at which the artist returned to the library.

Just then Phœbe and Amy entered, and Mr. Hammerton expressed great pleasure at seeing Miss Somerton.

Mr. Richard Tallant thought he saw in Amy's face, as she returned Mr. Hammerton's graceful salutation, an expression of love and admiration; but this might have originated out of what he had heard in the summer-house, and he felt annoyed in spite of himself, and without really knowing why.

"Shall we have our smoke?" he said, a little impatiently. "The ladies will excuse us, and we can walk outside on the grass."

"Presently, Mr. Tallant," said the young nobleman, entering into a conversation with Miss Tallant and Amy about a score of trifling things.

"Don't let us detain you, pray," said Miss
Tallant; and by-and-by Mr. Tallant and Mr.
Hammerton, with Mr. Phillips between them,
sauntered leisurely up and down the lawn,
whilst Phœbe returned to the new books.

Amy sat down near her, with "In Memoriam"
in her hand. The Laureate's sublime thoughts
had long since been in her heart, but she was
accustomed to dwell upon this greatest of all
his great works when her feelings were more
than usually agitated; and this morning sadness
and gladness were so commingled that she was
almost beside herself with a sense of doubt and
fear and sorrow, and of trembling joy and pre-
sentiments of dread and danger.

> " He past ; a soul of nobler tone :
>   My spirit loved and loves him yet,
>   Like some poor girl whose heart is set
> On one whose rank exceeds her own.

> " He mixing with his proper sphere,
>   She finds the baseness of her lot,
>   Half jealous of she knows not what,
> And envying all that meet him there.

The little village looks forlorn ;
　　She sighs amid her narrow days,
　　Moving about the household ways,
In that dark house where she was born.

"The oolish neighbours come and go,
　　And tease her till the day draws by;
　　At night she weeps ' How vain am I !
How should he love a thing so low ? ' "

Tears fell upon the page. Her inferior rank, her humble origin, made her love seem a vain and selfish thing indeed. She sometimes despised herself for permitting even the thought of it to have a place in her heart. And yet Cophetua made the beggar-maid his queen. But how beautiful she was!

Amy did not understand her own peculiar beauty, refined and toned as it was by the kindness of her nature, the vigour of her intellect, and the graces of her mind ; or she might not have despaired of the love of the next heir to the Earldom of Verner.

O, if he were but poor If he had even

been six or seven removes from an earldom; but to set her mind upon one so high! It was madness, and yet poor Amy could not choose but love; and Mr. Hammerton had been so marked in his courtesy towards her whenever he had seen her at the farm, or met her on his occasional visits to Barton Hall, that faint whispers of hope would sometimes cheer her heart.

Before Mr. Hammerton left he expressed a desire to see the garden. There were some famous flowers which he had heard Earl Verner's gardener speak of as rarities that he had seen at Barton Hall.

Miss Tallant volunteered to show Mr. Hammerton the garden, and insisted that Amy should accompany them.

"We will all go," said Mr. Tallant. "Come along, Mr. Phillips! you are interested in these things; for my part, I know little about them."

They saw the flowers and discussed their merits, and then, somehow or other, Mr. Hammerton found himself engaged in a deep conversation with Miss Tallant and Amy; and by-and-by he was alone with Miss Somerton, and he was all graciousness and gentle words then.

Once she felt his breath warm upon her cheek, and once he pressed her hand. She blushed, and the tears came into her eyes, why or wherefore she could not tell. And then Lionel pressed her hand again, and said what a delightful creature Miss Tallant was to leave him alone with her dear friend.

He gathered a rose and playfully hung it in her hair, and then he asked her if she remembered the poetic legend of the origin of the red rose. "Roses were all white originally when first they bloomed in Eden. Eve, when first she saw the beautiful flower, could not suppress her admiration, and in her joy at its beauty she stooped down and imprinted a kiss on its snowy bosom. The rose stole the scarlet tinge from her velvet lip, and wears it yet. So goes the story; I cannot give you the authority, but the tradition is poetic; is it not?"

Amy looked up and smiled, and Lionel knew that she loved him. The most secret page of her story was before him, and he read it with pride and satisfaction.

Lionel went on talking all kinds of loving trifles which in anyone else's mouth would have seemed ridiculous to Amy; but she could only weep at them and feel a strange fluttering at her heart as she listened to him and walked with him in the shadiest and most remote paths of the Barton Hall gardens.

In the evening Mr. Christopher Tallant returned from town, and was greatly surprised to find his son at Barton Hall; and equally astonished the next morning to find that he had risen for the morning mail, and gone back to London.

CHAPTER XII.

BENEATH THE GOWN.

PAUL SOMERTON had improved that friendship started at the Ashford Club, and had latterly dropped the evening society of Thomas Dibble. He had made the discovery in search of which Mr. Dibble had been useful to him, and since then he had preferred working at the mine alone.

Somehow or other the lad had acquired a relish for the work in which he was engaged. A desire to please his sister, whom he loved, had been strengthened by the dislike he had conceived for Mr. Gibbs. Had he known half as much of strange mysteries as the author of "Zanoni," he might have fancied that he was impelled by some secret sympathy or antipathy over which he had no control. But Paul knew very little even about the great novelist's romantic books, much less of Victor Cousin, Condillac and materialism, Jamblichus and Polinus, Swedenborg and Behemen, the golden ass of Apuleius and Hamilton's metaphysics ; and all he had ever heard of Puysegur and Mesmer was at a provincial lecture on Mesmerism and Biology by a quack, who amused his audience immensely with a couple of confederates.

So Paul never attempted to investigate the fascination which an exposure of Mr. Gibbs had for him, coupled with a vague sort of desire to save Mr. Richard Tallant and Mr. Hammerton from the machinations of so consummate a scoundrel. The sequel, however, may appear as if some secret power were at work to bring those two opposing forces, Paul Somerton and Shuffleton Gibbs, in contact.

He had watched at the club-door for some nights before Mr. Hammerton appeared again. He came at last, however, and Paul at once accosted him.

It had occurred to Paul previously that he would endeavour to watch the players until he openly detected Shuffleton's double cards, and then rush into the room and denounce him.

But this he thought would compromise the poor club-keeper's position, and was a little more showy and romantic than necessary. So Paul accosted the Hon. Mr. Hammerton, and as he did so Mr. Shuffleton Gibbs passed into the club, and noticed the incident.

Mr. Hammerton was impatient at first, but when Paul told him whom he was, his curiosity was aroused, and Paul's earnestness soon rivetted his attention.

"Not a very creditable part to play, my young friend, that of spy upon the conduct of your master and his friends, by-and-by," said Mr. Hammerton.

"If I do good thereby to my master?" said Paul, a little timidly, as the nature of his employ-ment struck him in the new light suggested by Mr. Hammerton.

"I think you have overstepped the bounds of both duty and prudence," said Mr. Hammerton.

"You may change your opinion," said Paul, more courageously. "I entered upon the business in your interest as well as Mr. Tallant's."

"Oh, indeed!" said Mr. Hammerton; "that was very kind of you, certainly. From whom did you receive your instructions?"

Paul did not reply; his pride was hurt, he had not expected such a reception as this.

"Suppose I inform Mr. Tallant how you have occupied yourself during these last few weeks?" said Mr. Hammerton; for *his* pride and dignity were hurt also, and he was offended at this interference with his liberty, in doubt for the moment whether Paul was a tool in more skilled hands.

"I shall watch no more, sir," said Paul. "You may take your own course; I have done my duty. You know how to test the truth of what I have told you. Good-night, sir."

Paul disappeared without another word, al-

though Mr. Hammerton called after him. He
felt miserably disappointed as he went home, and
could not help feeling that there was something
of the sneak in his composition, after all.

Why had he persevered so in this wretched
business? Why had he done so much more than
his sister had asked him to do? He would move
no further in it now.

After all his trouble, to be snubbed, and by the
gentleman most to be benefited! "Well, people
should mind their own business," he said to himself. "I'll mind mine in future."

It would have been better for Paul Somerton
had he resolved upon this when first he arrived in
London. It was hardly wise for his sister to
excite his curiosity to so high a pitch about the
conduct of other people. Both of them suffered
for their indiscretion—suffered in more ways than
one. Amy's object was, however, served in a
measure; for the dangerous career of young
Hammerton was cut short on this eventful night
of Paul's resolve to mind his own business in

future, though it would have been better for the honourable gentleman had the conclusion of his gaming experiences been less demonstrative than it was.

When Paul left him, he joined the little party at the Ashford Club, determined not to entertain suspicions which for the moment had been strongly aroused.

This was the night when the pigeon was to be completely plucked. Clever manipulators in this art do not seize upon their prey at a first, or a second, or a third interview. They lure Signor Pigeon on by degrees. They let him win in the first encounter, and in the second or third vary the luck, exciting him at last, perchance, by a rather heavy loss, which he is anxious to retrieve. Shuffleton Gibbs had worked Mr. Hammerton to this point, and had been assisted to some extent by Mr. Richard Tallant; but the latter gentleman had been the tool rather than the confederate of his University companion.

University companion! It was this educational

position which made Gibbs tolerated in the society which he affected. He was a University man, if he had not taken a degree. Something happened to disgrace him a little at Christ Church, it is true; but there!—"it was only a bit of wickedness." He made love to a pastrycook's daughter, and ran away with her, or something of the sort, and had a row with a fellow-student over cards. What was all this? Youthful indiscretion, an exuberance of animal spirits. He was a gentleman by education, at all events; he had worn a gown.

That would have been enough to have made him a man of consideration in any provincial city in the empire, and it was a great passport even in cosmopolitan London; but in the dear old cathedral city where Arthur Phillips lived, what weight it would have given to Mr. Gibbs! "Of what college?" says a simpering inquirer. "Christ Church," is the reply, and the man's position is made. You had better be hanged than not have worn a gown in some English cities.

And so the gown assisted to cover the cloven hoofs of Mr. Shuffleton Gibbs, even in London; the gown had been sufficient for Richard Tallant, though it had not been enough for his father, and it had not shielded all the owner's villanies; it had nevertheless worked favourably with Mr. Hammerton, who had put down Shuffleton's wild college career to his dashing character, his natural wilfulness, and his animal spirits.

But during that last evening when Signor Pigeon was being plucked, the gown somehow fell aside, and Mr. Hammerton, made hot and suspicious by the loss of more than his present fortune, and something on account of his money in perspective, suddenly bounced out of his seat, picked up a duplicate card, seized Gibbs by the collar, and called him "cheat" and "black-leg."

There was a terrible row, you may be sure. Gibbs, in the strong grip of Mr. Hammerton, shrunk like a coward, as he was, despite his college reputation as a "fast" man.

Clubmen and waiters thronged round the pair,

and Mr. Shuffleton Gibbs' conviction was complete; for, besides another duplicate turning up, the cards were found to be "doctored" substitutes for those used at the club. Fortunately for Richard Tallant, he had "cut out" of the four who were playing an hour before this *contretemps* occurred. His conduct was not without some suspicion in the club; but his father's reputation, his own presumed wealth, and his generally open and apparently honest outspoken sentiments, protected him from anything beyond mere suspicion.

He neither attacked nor defended his friend Gibbs, but looked on whilst several members of the Ashford conducted Mr. Gibbs to the door and thrust him into the street. A confederate assisted in the expulsion, and was loudest, after his colleague's disappearance, in his condemnation of all such scoundrels.

"A plague on all cowards, I say, and a vengeance, too. . . . . A bad world, I say! I would I were a weaver; I could sing psalms or anything. A plague of all cowards, I say still."

Falstaff was not more demonstrative in praise of virtue, and against cowardice, than this wretched colleague of Gibbs' in expressions of utter disgust for cheats and black-legs. Mr. Richard Tallant was even bold enough to sneer at the ranter, and advise him to communicate his sentiments to Shuffleton personally.

Meanwhile, Mr. Gibbs, shaking himself for a moment like a dog after a swim, quietly re-adjusted his crumpled collar, and deliberately pulled on his unimpeachable lavender gloves.

If you could have seen his face, you would have noticed the thin lips closely compressed, and the little eyes fixed and glaring. There were no great signs of rage there; but an expression of disappointment—not of despair by any means. He had been in difficulties before, and was not wont to lose his coolness; but he had never had "cheat" and "black-leg" thrown in his teeth until now, nor ever before trembled in the grip of an adversary. He wondered now at his own cowardice, and clenched his little gloved-hand as he walk through St. James's Park, and nursed his wicked thoughts.

By-and-by he lit a cigar, and walked musingly along, looking up at the moon. A reader for the daily press going homewards after his day's work, looked at him, and put him down for a sentimental swell, planning a plot for a poem, or rehearsing some great scene for a new novel.

How clever we all are in reading character! Let us hope the poor newspaper fag read his proofs better than he read Shuffleton Gibbs.

CHAPTER XIII.

DESCRIBES A GREAT FINANCIAL STORM AND
EXHIBITS THOMAS DIBBLE IN A NEW CHA-
RACTER.

IT came steadily but surely, gently at first,
like great storms come, with a gradual lowering
of the clouds and a gradual increase in the wind.
It began in a calm—a quiet, happy, pleasant calm
—a calm that may be typified by a man seated
on the lawn at Barton, and smoking in the shade,
with sheep bleating at a distance.

It came out of a calm, we say—a delightful
time of rising markets, when the bulls of the Stock
Exchange were in clover, and the bears at fault.
It began when most kinds of shares were at a
premium ; when all sorts of companies were
paying big dividends, and 5*l.* shares were selling
at 8*l.* and 10*l.*; when everything was " looking

up;" when men bought to invest, and even bought one day to sell the next at a profit. First, there was a whisper from the Continent which agitated the financial atmosphere for a moment—the first breeze of the coming storm. The bears sniffed it, but the bulls feared it not; and shares for a moment wavered, only to recover and make the calm seem all the more assuring. Then a whisper came from the New World, and there was an Atlantic roughness about it at which the bears opened their nostrils and sniffed with a hungry relish. The bulls wavered still in doubt, and then in a sudden darkness the big clouds gathered, and the wind blew a hurricane—blew tempestuously from the shores of France, with tributary winds from Austria and Prussia, and local winds from St. Stephen's. Then the bears growled and frisked and bit and bellowed, and the bulls fought hard and butted with their horns; but the bears tore and lacerated them: for the financial storm had come, and there was panic everywhere. The Genii of Finance no longer in the sun looked hideous and fearful, and the magicians who had hitherto controlled them had lost their power, because the world had faith in them no longer. The story is not new; it crops up afresh once in about every eight or ten years.

The newspapers did not describe the storm as we have described it. They conveyed the intelligence in technical terms which made it hard and biting :—"Orientals are now at $1\frac{1}{4}$ to $1\frac{1}{8}$ dis.; Credits, 1 to $\frac{7}{8}$; Unity shares have declined to 8 to $7\frac{1}{2}$ dis.; Imperials have gone to $5\frac{1}{8}$ to $4\frac{3}{8}$ dis.; Discount Company, $\frac{3}{8}$ to $\frac{1}{4}$ dis.; Overton, Baker and Co.'s Bank, $\frac{7}{8}$ to $\frac{3}{4}$ dis. The railway market continues dull, with a downward tendency; there is a further reduction of $\frac{1}{4}$ to $\frac{1}{2}$ per cent. in Great Western, South Eastern, Great Eastern, and Great Northerns.

"Another serious failure is reported from Liverpool, and the directors of the Bank of England have to-day raised the minimum rate of discount from 6 to 7 per cent."

This was the fragmentary way in which the

newspapers indicated the financial storm, and the figures started up in the night, like fiends, haunting the pillows of many a man, in town and in country, who had been induced to "speculate" in a few finance and other shares "just to make a little money"—men who had never touched shares before, and did not even know the "beastly" title affixed to professional buyers and sellers on the Stock Exchange. To them a bull meant an animal that was dangerous in the fields, and grand at agricultural shows; and a bear was an ugly brute that climbed up a pole at the Zoological Gardens. William Jones the grocer and Timothy Robinson the draper, who had been induced to buy a few Overtons, or Orientals, at 3 premium, in the hope of selling at 5 or 6 premium before the half-yearly meeting, were nothing more than bulls, nevertheless, in Stock Exchange phraseology, and only to become despondent and miserable bears at 5 or 10 discount.

"Been bulling the market, Mithter Dibble? Pray explain yourself, and don't offend a

woman's thenthibilities by such terms as that,"
said Mrs. Thomas Dibble, leaning back in her
chair, and vainly endeavouring to thread a
needle.

" Bulling means selling, my love," said Thomas,
trembling; " selling shares without having them,
you see, and——"

" Mithter Dibble, it isn't as I wish to be severe
on you, but I begin to suspect you are drunk, thir!
——drunk, drunk, drunk," said Mrs. Dibble, laying down her needle in despair, and rapping the
table with her thimble.

" You may call I what you likes," said Dibble,
with a tremendous effort to be bold; " but I'm
sober enough. I wishes I were drunk."

" Good heaventh! why, whath come to the
man? How dare you wish you were drunk, thir
—how dare you, thir!"

" Dare? I tell you, Maria, I'm a miserable
bull, a dead-beat bull, as ever was," said Dibble,
weeping.

" You're a beast, if that's what you mean," said

L 2

Mrs. Dibble, convinced that her Thomas was intoxicated.

But Dibble was only suffering from the panic. He had been tempted by the financial sunshine— and Mr. Shuffleton Gibbs — and had bought the shares of a company that had made a call and failed, and of another whose shares had fallen from 10l. a share to 5l. worse than nothing. It had been brought about in this wise: Mr. Gibbs was indebted to Mr. Dibble for many little acts of courtesy and attention, as a visitor to Mr. Richard Tallant at the Iron Company's offices. Thomas had always a chair and a polite submissive word for Mr. Gibbs, and so one day that gentleman, arguing correctly that Mr. Dibble must have saved a few hundred pounds, kindly showed that confiding porter how to make a few hundreds more ; and Mr. Thomas Dibble, in the simplicity of his nature, became a bull, without the knowledge of his better-half. Whispers of the panic had come into the big company's offices where Thomas portered it, and at last he began to understand that his five hundred pounds were tossed about in the storm, and liable to be sunk and lost for ever; and on the day in question, when Thomas went home and confessed that he was a bull in a panic, and other similarly insane things, Mr. Gibbs had explained to him his position, and advised him to consider his money lost for the present, but consoling him with stories of the immense losses which other people had suffered.

" Mr. Gibbs advised me to do it," said Dibble.

" Do what, you fool?" shouted Mrs. Dibble, who lost all patience with him.

" Speckerlate with the five hundred pounds which we had at the bank," said Thomas.

" We had—*we* had, Miththter Dibble: it wath my own money, Thomath, and you have never dared to touch it?" said Mrs. D., her face white and her eyes flashing.

" I touched it to make a thousand of it, Maria; that were my full intention."

"Oh, you monthter! Oh, Dibble, Dibble! Oh,

Thomath, Thomath! I thee it all—you have lost the money!"

" Ise afraid on it, that I be," said Dibble. " The bull sells, and the bear buys. 'If you bear the market now,' Mr. Gibbs says, 'you may get right;' but, oh Lord! oh dear, Maria! Ise quite lost! What be I to do? what be I to do?"

Poor Dibble lifted up his arms, and looked appealingly towards his furious wife, who sunk back in her chair with a scream for water. The wretched bull, glad of any diversion from the main point, rushed to his wife's assistance. She had really fainted, this strong-minded Mrs. Dibble, who could think for everybody, and conduct the government of the country if necessary.

She had often said that had she been a man she would have been in Parliament; and not only in Parliament, but a cabinet minister. There was nothing too high for the giant intellect of this domineering wife of poor Thomas Dibble; and yet here she lay like a dead thing, with her cap on the floor, her arms lying helplessly by her side, and Dibble bathing her face, at the loss of five hundred pounds. But it was the insubordination of Dibble which affected her more than the loss of the money, and when she came to herself again, wet and soddened, she declared she would never forgive him.

"Never, Thomath, tho don't athk it; ith not ath I bear malithe, nor am mean, but for a woman who hath loved like me, and refuthed the greatetht offerth from noblemen—I say, for one who gave her heart up ath I did, it ith not in nature to forgive thuch detheption as yourth, Thomath Dibble. How true it ith, ath it ith written, that the heart of man ith dethperately wicked."

And Mrs. Dibble went to bed with her woes, locked her door, and left the wretched Thomas to bemoan his unhappy lot in darkness and in the kitchen, where he fell asleep by-and-by, and dreamed that he was a bull being devoured by a horde of bears; but he awoke, and found that he was only in danger of being eaten by crickets and beetles, which held great meetings on the

Dibbleonian hearth-stone every night. They were no doubt greatly astonished to find poor Thomas lying there all his length ; for their investigation of him was very minute, much more so than Thomas liked, who jumped upon his feet, and roared and kicked until Mrs. Dibble, certain of thieves and murder, opened the window, and cried " Fire ! " and then, being a strong-minded woman, jumped into bed, and covered her head with the bed-clothes.

Happily, Paul Somerton came home just in time to put matters right, and induce Mrs. Dibble to admit Thomas to her room, at least for her own protection. Poor Dibble said next day he would rather have slept with the beetles ; he was sure he should have been happier in the kitchen, after all.

Meanwhile the storm in the City was raging, and spreading far away to all points of the compass. Though the moon shone forth calmly, on Cornhill and Lombard-street, on Threadneedle-street and on the Stock Exchange, through all the night the storm raged in men's hearts; it tossed men and women on their beds, and shook giants of finance where they lay sleepless and afeared: it tore along the railways, sealed up in letters, which carried the tempest to Liverpool, Manchester, Sheffield, Bristol, Birmingham, and even to the cathedral city where Mr. Phillips resided. They were like so many Pandora's boxes, these letters from the City the next morning, letting out on being opened evils without end. Despair and ruin were in many of them, and all the country was agitated with fear. If an invading host had been sailing up the Thames, the consternation would not have been so great; for the people could have gone forth and done battle with the foe. But there is no fighting a financial storm,—no contending with Stock Exchange terrors.

After the arrival of Pandora's letters, there went forth into the country flights of telegrams,— electric pigeons which settled in crowds with their missives in all the towns of England, and the storm increased tenfold with the excitement of the electric current.

During the morning hundreds of bulls put on bear's clothing, and the shares of Overton, Baker, & Co., began to fall; and in the afternoon the leading discount-house in the country gave way to the pressure: and then fresh flights of electric pigeons went forth into the towns that Overton, Baker, & Co., had failed for ten millions of money.

You may fancy that this panic bears a strong likeness to the one which has only recently occurred. Panics are closely akin, and therefore much alike. If the crash of 1866 enables you the better to realise that which forms part of the present history, so much the better. Thomas Dibble will never forget in which panic he lost his wife's five hundred pounds, and how he suffered by his mad efforts to replace the money.

CHAPTER XIV.

ARTHUR PHILLIPS AT WORK.

He sat near the trunk of an oak-tree, and a brook made murmuring music amongst the gnarled and grey and knotty old roots. There were big burdock-leaves at his feet, trailing brambles full of luscious fruit, and thick brown and yellow grasses.

Beneath the branches of the tree, on one side, there was a peep of distant tender hills, with a foreground of foliage just tinted with autumnal touches of red and yellow. He sat in the shadow of a clump of grand old Severnshire elms, and on his right at some distance a number of farm labourers were stacking wheat.

It was a bright, sunny afternoon in the latter part of August, and the sun played amongst the leaves of the old oak-tree, keeping the artist's eye and hand rapidly at work. And never had Arthur Phillips watched the sunny gleams with more intense interest. A tramp with his slovenly wife, wandering out of the footpath to find a cool shelter for rest, stood to look at the artist for a moment; and a couple of school-boys, who had been fishing for minnows in the adjacent brook, sat down quietly in the grass, and lazily watched the glowing canvas.

It would have made a pretty picture this, of the artist and his spectators. But Phillips was soon alone again; he was too severe and earnest for the school-boys. A squirrel ventured to peep at him from a branch in the oak-tree, and a couple of mice whisked by him, and squeaked beneath the leaves of the broad burdock. A stupid moth lit upon the wet stump of his painted tree and spoiled its pretty wings.

How quiet, how peaceful it was, how thoroughly the country! By-and-by Arthur leaned back on his camp-stool and thought so; and his heart was grateful for the running brook, the whispering trees, the broad expanse of distant hills and meadows, and above all for the sympathy which he possessed in his own nature for the beautiful and sublime. The sun disappeared behind a cloud for a few minutes, leaving the oak-tree almost in its own natural colour, and showing the artist's successful touches. However far short of the reality, the canvas held some wonderful sunny effects : the leaves of the grand old tree were fairly illuminated, as if gleams of sunshine had gone through them, indicating almost the fibres of the lower branches.

No man knew how far art is below nature ; no painter felt more the inferiority of a picture when compared with the ever-changing and always beautiful reality : but Arthur Phillips knew when he had achieved something beyond the ordinary work, and he was pleased that his labour on this occasion had been successful ; for Arthur was now actually painting for money. He had long since ceased to accept commissions, except for subjects of his own selection, and had painted more for the love of his art than for what his art would bring. The drudgery of painting had been got over long ago: the years of patient industry and unrewarded toil; the pictures returned from the Academy unhung; the adverse criticism when at last they were hung: all this had long since been at an end, and Arthur Phillips left to select his subjects and name his own price for his pictures.

But on this bright day in August the artist sat once more hard at work, painting for money, painting for subsistence. For not only had he been induced to invest largely in Overton, Baker, & Co., but he had a deposit account at their local branch in his native city of Severntown, and the branch had succumbed to the same monetary pressure which had swamped the head concern. And Arthur Phillips was nearly penniless.

There were many others in Severntown almost in the same condition, and from the same cause. So Arthur, instead of making himself wretched and miserable, packed up his box of colours, and went out to finish that bit of local study upon which we find him engaged, prior to locking himself up in his study for months of hard work.

"I thought I should find you at last, old boy," said Mr. Hammerton, putting his hand familiarly on Arthur's shoulders. "By the aid of your man, that faithful old grinder of colours and cleaner of pallettes, I traced you to the cross-roads; there I was at fault, and almost gave you up. I believe my old mare scented you out at last."

"Then give my best thanks to the old mare, for I am glad to see you," said Arthur.

"By Jove, that's pretty! what a glorious bit of colour! Have you finished?"

"Yes; I think so."

"Then pack up—here, I'll help you—and let us have a quiet chat. Your man said he was to meet you here in about an hour, to carry the things home."

"Yes," said Arthur; "but I have finished. I was just thinking of smoking a quiet pipe whilst the sun goes down."

" Bravo ! we'll mingle our smoke together, friend Arthur," said Hammerton ; adding, a little more seriously, " and our tears, too, by Jove ! It's the last time we shall see each other for a long time, I guess."

"Indeed ! Why ?" said Arthur, turning the key in his colour-box.

" I'm off to foreign lands, Arthur—

'Anywhere, anywhere, out of the world.' "

" Are you serious, Lionel ?"

" I was never more so. I have had a few angry words with my brother ; and though he's a good fellow, and is sorry for what he has said, I must go away for a time."

Arthur looked up inquiringly.

" The fact is, I have been a great fool ; I have lost a lot of money lately. I don't know how it was, but through young Tallant I was induced to visit the Ashford Club. You have not heard, then, of the row at that quiet, but now notorious, institution ?"

"No; I never heard of the Ashford before."

"Why, it was in all the papers, man,—about a fellow cheating, and being put out into the street. My name was mentioned. You shall see the paper. Well, all that naturally annoyed my brother; but, to clinch matters, I was advised to buy a lot of Overton and Baker's shares, to put myself right, and I have gone all to the bad. Overton and Bakers have failed, and I not only lose the value of the shares, but there is a liability, and a large one, besides. I suppose you heard of the failure?"

"Yes. I had a large deposit with them at Severntown," said Arthur.

"You had? By Jove! I'm sorry for that. And you are hit then, too; much, Arthur?"

"Yes, considerably. I must work hard, and make it up again."

"I'm awfully sorry. But there, cheer up, old boy; there is no good in worrying about it, I suppose."

" No," said Arthur, quietly. " And where are you going, Lionel ? "

" To join my regiment at Bombay ; I am to be gazetted next week. I'm not going in bad disgrace, Arthur—don't think that ; but my brother, the Earl, twitted me with my folly and my expenditure, you know, and, no doubt, he was right. I have been a fool. A few years in the army will do a fellow good. There is no chance of war ; that's unfortunate."

They chatted and smoked until Arthur's man came and carried the artist's picture and materials away, and then they strolled together towards a farm where Lionel had put up his horse, and where Arthur had arranged to sleep.

In the farmer's clean-sanded parlour, Lionel told Arthur the story of his losses, not forgetting the incident of his interview with Paul Somerton. This, it seemed, had annoyed Lionel as much as anything in the whole of the unfortunate affair. He was satisfied that Miss Somerton had set her brother to watch him.

"I could never have supposed that a girl could have behaved so absurdly. You may rely upon it, Arthur, that pretty bailiff's daughter had set her mind on marrying me, and she was anxious that I should not get through my patrimony without her assistance, I suppose. Imagine the absurdity of the thing! The girl fancies I am in love with her."

"You have paid her great attention," said Arthur.

"Who doesn't pay a pretty girl great attention, whoever she may be?" said Lionel.

"You were in raptures with her picture—not out of compliment to the artist, but to the pretty face—the aristocratic head," said Arthur, significantly.

"Ah, you have anticipated me: I shall want that picture," said Lionel, with assumed indifference; "but imagine a bailiff's daughter setting her heart upon the next heir to the earldom of Verner, and making her brother a spy upon him lest he should lose too much money at cards. By Jove, Arthur, it was an impudent thing to do."

M 2

" Did she do it ? "

" Did she ? Of course she did. Why, the impudent young blackguard told me who he was, as if he had some claim upon me."

" And so he had, if he was warning you against conspirators."

" Look at it in that light, perhaps he had ; but what about the other view ? "

" She is a fine, handsome girl, Miss Somerton, and accomplished ; she's fit for the wife of a prince," said Arthur, in his quiet, emphatic manner.

" Why, what radicalism you are talking ! Marry a bailiff's daughter to a prince ? "

" A prince might be proud of such a wife as Amy Somerton. You have not seen so much of her as I have, and you may rely upon it you have wronged her."

" She's an impudent, meddling baggage, Arthur —a presumptuous, designing woman," said Lionel, with an angry flash of the eye.

" I don't think so, indeed," said Arthur.

"I am sure; therefore we will not discuss the point further. Miss Tallant would be a better theme."

But Arthur Phillips would not talk about Phœbe: and so at last they parted, Lionel shaking Arthur by the hand, and telling him that whatever might come to pass, he should never forget the many happy hours they had passed together, and that he should always treasure his friendship. Arthur was not behindhand in reciprocating Lionel's kind feelings and expressions, and he stood at the farmer's gate and watched his aristocratic friend until he had ridden out of sight.

> "Now came still evening on, and twilight grey
> Had in her sober livery all things clad."

With all his love of nature, with all his courage, Arthur Phillips felt sadly lonely now, as he stood listening to the last sound of the clatter of Lionel's horse's hoofs on the white, hard road.

It seemed as if all things that he loved faded out, or were unattainable. He had formed a warm attachment for Lionel Hammerton, and he would miss his cheery voice in the cathedral close at Severntown. Arthur, indeed, had no other familiar friend. He had followed his art with such singleness of purpose, that his life had been comparatively solitary, and he knew little or nothing of the world and its doings ; hence his likes and dislikes were intensified.

For the last two or three years his love for Phœbe Tallant had grown up into a passion which he could not control, and it was only this which disturbed the peaceful course of his life. He had never thought of disclosing his feelings to her. It had been a great relief to him to tell Lionel Hammerton, and more particularly when he had for a moment feared that he had a rival in his friend. Not that Arthur, perhaps, ought to have looked upon any one as a rival, when marriage could hardly be said to have entered his thoughts. To be near his love, to see her often, to speak to her, to dwell on her kind words, that was enough for Arthur. His ambitiou so far had soared no higher. How could he, a poor, ill-shaped little fellow, with his solitary life, ask a fair, bright thing like Phœbe Tallant to throw in her lot with his—with his, the paid tutor?

No, poor Arthur! he had never arrived at such a daring pitch of passion and presumption, even when he had a large balance at his bankers, with which to meet, in some fashion, the monetary consideration of the wealthy father. If he had known more of the world he might have ventured to make this last cast of the die; but a quiet, retiring, modest, susceptible nature like Arthur's, wont to brood over all sorts of imaginary nothings, wont to dream and set his thoughts upon the quiet river, to be wafted out far away beyond the world, it was impossible for him to tell Mr. Tallant that he had fallen in love with his daughter.

Once or twice he had thought there was something mean in his position at Barton Hall; that he had taken a mean advantage of his position as tutor to fall in love with his pupil. This idea

had taken such fast possession of him at one time
that he had almost determined to leave the
country; but his will was not strong enough to
shut out Phœbe from his sight. He was a prisoner to her charms, and content to remain so.
How his excitement had blurted out his captivity
to Lionel Hammerton was something that he
could hardly understand himself; but he was glad
that he had no longer to carry the secret about
alone : it was like a divided responsibility now
that Lionel knew it.

"And so I am to begin again," he thought.
"Well so be it; maybe this is but a kind act of
mercy to give me more to think about. I have
been lazy; I will paint a grand picture."

CHAPTER XV.

THE trees were covered with a hundred shades
of brown and red and yellow. A pleasant Sep-
tember breeze wandered about, carrying with it
here and there the report of the sportsman's gun.
Flocks of sheep cropped the sweet herbage, and
crowds of happy-looking gleaners gathered the
stray ears of wheat which Mr. Somerton had left
in the corn-fields.

There had been an abundant harvest, and the
corn was well and successfully garnered. The
big yellow stacks peered out amongst the trees
round about the Hall farm, and Luke Somerton
sat cozily smoking his after-dinner pipe.

Peace and plenty was the prevailing characteristic of the place, and Luke Somerton was on particularly good terms, at the moment, with himself and all the world.

"I wonder how Paul is getting on," he said, musingly, just as his wife had folded up the table-cloth and instructed her servant to "get those dinner-things washed up at once."

"Oh, he'll get on well enough," said Mrs. Somerton, "if his sister doesn't spoil him with her pack of silly letters. One would think they had nothing in the world to do but to write letters to each other."

"Well, there's no harm in their writing to each other; it may keep Paul out of mischief."

"He is getting very little money for his age; he ought to have enough to keep him without assistance from us by this time. It's little we save."

"You think too much about saving money, Sarah. There are lots of things in life better than money."

"You may say what you please, Luke, the

great object of life should be to make money and get position. If one cannot gain it oneself, we should try to get it through our children," said Mrs. Somerton, taking up her knitting and sitting by the window.

A stranger wandering about the quiet, peaceful, happy-looking country of which we speak in the opening of this chapter, would assuredly not have looked for the expression of such worldly views by the mistress of that comfortable-looking house amongst the trees. The thought passed over the farmer's mind, but so lightly that he did not attempt to give expression to it, though his reply bordered slightly upon it.

"And what do you call position, Sarah? Has it anything to do with happiness ' asked Luke.

"Position! Why, to be above other people. To be looked up to instead of being looked down upon. To have servants of one's own, and not be servants ourselves."

"That is, your husband should be something

more than a farm bailiff, or a farmer even on his own account. The old story; it's no use, Sarah, we can't alter our lot. It seems to me that a clear conscience, and owing nobody a penny, is about the best position in the world, after all,' whatever your station in life."

"I know that is your opinion, Luke, and there's something in it, for those who like to jog through the world and be nothing to nobody. We have money now, and why can't we have a farm of our own, at least?"

"Oh, we've had enough of farming on our own account, Sarah. These are not the days for farmers with small incomes. It doesn't suit me to be peddling about in the old style of farming. I have gone in for the science of the thing, and I must have the best machinery to work with; and you want a big holding for that and lots of capital besides. We are much better off as it is. Mr. Tallant is rich, and, although he gets now a fair return for his money, he's sunk a lot in this estate."

"And what for? That young Tallant will soon get through it all."

"Stop until he inherits."

"Ah, there will be changes here whenever the old man goes. Whatever will become of Phœbe? I shall take it upon myself to speak to him about that young lady."

"I should think you'll do nothing of the sort."

"Why not? I say it is a burning shame to keep her mewed up here. She would pick up a duke, at least, in London; and, as sure as fate, that little painter fellow will get her if she stays at Barton much longer."

"You seem to be quite insane upon this subject, Sarah."

"Oh yes, of course. Everything that *you* can't see through is absurd; it always was so, Luke. When you have got as far as the end of your nose there is an end to your prospect, unless you are thinking about what crop should follow wheat or barley."

" Now, then ; get into a passion. You said you would talk quietly if I would stay."

" I am not in a passion—nothing of the kind," said Mrs. S., knitting at double-quick speed.

" Very well, then, mind you don't get into a passion," said Luke, smiling.

" Phœbe Tallant was made to shine in society, and to marry well ; and it is horrible to see wealth and power going out of a young girl's grasp just because nobody puts her anywhere near the prize."

" Happiness never seems to form part of your philosophy, Sarah."

" Wealth and power, Luke—isn't that happiness ? To wear real diamonds, and heaps of them ; to drive in the parks ; to be presented at court ; to make other women envy you. Happiness ! Talk of clear consciences and all that stuff, to set a room full of women hating you for your wealth and beauty is bliss—joy above everything !"

Luke took his pipe from his mouth and gazed in astonishment at his wife, who had ceased knitting, and was looking out beyond where he sat,—but not at the quiet rural picture spread out before her. She was simply looking at her own thoughts.

"Women, Luke, are devils. To men they are bad enough, but they treat each other like fiends : they are mean to an extent beyond all imagination ; they hate each other mortally ; and a pretty·woman is a mark for all their spite and slander. But she takes it out ; she has her revenge ; she stings them like an adder."

"You are a strange woman, Sarah ; but you say a great deal more than you believe," said Luke.

"Do I ? I believe women capable of anything. But men deserve to be deceived by them, because the first of the race was a sneak and a coward. 'The woman tempted me, and I did eat.'"

Mrs. Somerton gave a contemptuous toss of her head, and went on with her knitting.

"What a pity you didn't marry some great gun who could have given you your full swing of power and wealth. You were a fine showy woman when I married you, Sarah; and hang me if you wouldn't eclipse some of the young ones now. What a blessing it would be if you hadn't such a bitter tongue."

Luke seemed to be turning this over in his mind, and contemplating it. He spoke half admiringly, half in regret.

"Ah, Luke, I dare say you think I am a fiend like the rest of my sex, and I feel like one at times; but if my time had to come over again, I should not alter my choice. There are some things that I've done which I would undo if I could, but not that, not that, Luke."

"Come, Sarah, that does me good," said Luke, going up to her, and putting his hand on her shoulders. "I have often thought we were an ill-assorted couple, and you've said many an unkind thing; but you have been a good wife to me after all, always done your duty—ay, and more; and I am sure your heart's in the right place."

Mrs. Somerton looked up at her husband with a disturbed expression of face. Her heart was in the right place; but her life was blighted by one act of wicked deceit, and she had struggled ever since to justify it to her conscience.

"There, you may go now, Luke. You don't believe I am so bad as I seem?"

"You're a good soul; try and drop all that nonsense about position, and we shall be a regular Darby and Joan in our old age."

Luke kissed her on the forehead and went out; and the wife continued her knitting.

There were some things that she would undo if she could! The years of secret hopes and fears, and doubts and misery, revealed in this expression, were not even dreamed of by Luke Somerton. She had schemed, and plotted, and built castles in the future, and carried about with her a big, burning secret, and it had lately begun to dawn upon her that her designs would be frustrated.

There may be far-seeing readers of this book

who have already plucked out the heart of Mrs. Somerton's mystery. We have made no great effort to conceal it from this piercing foresight. It is no new thing that we have invented. Our story will not be injured by your knowing Mrs. Somerton's secret from the beginning, neither will it be particularly enhanced by delaying the disclosure of the great plot of her married life.

But there are other things crowding upon my attention, and we must leave Mrs. Somerton at present without further explanation, to chafe against the bars of her own self-made prison-house.

CHAPTER XVI.

MAY BE SAID TO INAUGURATE A SERIES OF
IMPORTANT CHANGES IN THE LIVES OF
SEVERAL NOTABLE PERSONS IN THIS HISTORY.

THE financial storm had been but little felt,
you see, at Barton Hall, or Mr. and Mrs. Somerton
would no doubt have said something about it in
the conversation which is set down in the previous
chapter.

Phœbe Tallant and her friend, Miss Somerton,
had read of it in the daily papers, which arrived
in a special parcel from Smith & Sons every day
at the nearest railway station, where a groom was
in waiting for them. But Phœbe and Amy knew
little or nothing about panics. It was to them
very much like what it was to the boy,—"something in the City." Miss Tallant's clever governess,

however, knew a great deal about a Panic, which she seemed to stroke and pat on the back in her intellectual superiority.

They little knew how seriously such a storm might affect the master of Barton Hall. It had already demolished more than one or two establishments of nearly equal importance; but Mr. Tallant was particularly strong in the back, as they say in the City, and it was well for him that such was the case, as was speedily exemplified soon after the first shock of the panic had vibrated throughout the country.

On the very day after the clever governess's description of a panic, the half-yearly meeting of the Eastern Banking Company (of which Mr. Tallant was chairman, and his son a director) was held at the London Tavern.

At about two o'clock quite a little crowd of anxious-looking people ascended the stone staircase, and entered that long room with the misty looking pictures in it and the great chandelier.

Some of the men were talking in loud whispers about the losses of the company and its evident mismanagement. There appeared to be a general feeling prevailing that it would be an awkward day for the directors. But this was no novelty at that time for directors of many other concerns. Gentlemen who had been working for years up to directorships, and some of whom had thought it necessary to obtain seats in the House of Commons, with a leading idea in this direction, now began to find that there were two sides to the directoral picture.

The time had been when a gentleman could materially augment his income by having a seat at various boards of management; the time had been when he not only got thereby a first-rate investment for the nominal sum which gave him the qualification for certain directorates, but when his social and commercial position were largely exalted by these appointments. But directors at this period, with a commercial panic in the City and throughout the kingdom, began to find their seats full of thorns, and pins, and needles, and everything but curled hair and feathers.

Shareholders in almost every shaky concern were down upon the directors, and in many instances very properly so; for gentlemen of repute, honourable men hitherto, had been weak enough to append their names to prospectuses and statements which they knew little or nothing about; and in some cases this was knavishly and cruelly done,—knavishly and cruelly, because honest and industrious people were induced to invest hard-earned savings in rotten schemes made to look safe by the names of the gentlemen who figured as directors. Sir This, and the Hon. the Other, Lord That, and Mr. This, M.P. for so and so, did not scruple to lend their names to designing villains who plundered the public behind these swellmarks, and in more than one case Sir This and Mr. That did not scruple to go shares in the booty.

So you see the times were rather out of joint for directorships, and many eminent City and country gentlemen would have been rejoiced could they all at once have quietly retired from their several boards of management without inquiry or explanation. Mr. Richard Tallant could have told you of several safes where shares and scrip had been lately locked away by strong-backed men with a firm resolution not to look into those safes for many months to come. Some of these shares had been bought at heavy premiums, and now all that remained were the frightful responsibilities which attached to them. But there always had been panics, people said, and there always would be ; and there always have been financial wreckers and sharpers to take advantage of monetary storms, and will be until the end.

The half-yearly report stated that a loss of 100,000*l.* had fallen upon the Bombay branch ; but this was by no means the worst feature in the affair, according to the views of the share-holders. Their shares, 100*l.* paid up, were quoted on the Stock Exchange at 5*l.* 10*s.*

The chairman explained that there was no *bonâ*

fide reason for this, the bank being not only solvent, but having 150,000*l.* to the good, and better advices were expected from India.

Mr. Tallant's was a long, clear, and honest statement, but it did not allay the storm of abuse which had been prepared for the directory.

One speaker called for the resignation of the chairman, and was applauded; another condemned the directory as a body, called upon them all to resign; another fell foul of the auditors; another said the managers of the branches were evidently a set of incompetent men, put in by favouritism.

By-and-by the first speaker, a City man of repute, and famous amongst companies as a financial orator, alluded to the fall in their shares, and attributed the depreciation to the conduct of one of the shareholders.

"Yes, gentlemen," he said, "one of our own firm,—one of our partners in this great concern,— has not only been the chief means of running the shares down, but he has profited by it; he has sold shares which do not exist, and bought those which timid people have thrown upon the market; he has borrowed shares for the purpose of depreciation, and——"

The speaker was interrupted for a moment by cries of "Name! name!" but he was an orator, and he had more to say before he had worked up his theme to the grand climax of naming the victim, whom he was pinning down with his long rhetorical lance.

"Gentlemen, this speculator—to call him by a mild name—is one of a very small but dangerous set of men, who have been engaged in rigging the market and damaging great and flourishing concerns—like wreckers, putting out false lights, and then plundering the unhappy mariners."

Cries of "Shame!" and "Name!" and "Swindler!" interrupted the speaker, who waved his hand for silence.

"I had hoped to have seen this gentleman here to-day; he ought to have been amongst us; I gave him notice that *I* should be here."

This elicited a cry of "Bravo!" and then the chairman rose to deprecate personalities. He feared the honorable proprietor was losing his discretion by excitement.

"Not so, Mr. Chairman," replied the honorable proprietor. "I am not speaking on the spur of the moment: my words are not born of mere excitement, sir. I have thought much and deeply about the remarks I am now making; nay more, I have taken advice upon them—they have gone through the legal crucible. (Cheers, "Bravo!" and confusion.) It is exceedingly hurtful to my own feelings to bring so painful a subject before this meeting, but I am prepared to sacrifice self, upon an occasion of this kind, to public duty."

"Hear, hear!" said several shareholders, whilst others murmured "Quite right."

"I have ample proof of the charge which I am making; and shall I not for the credit and honour and safety of the trading community of this great city, in a time of such financial danger, unmask the dastard before the eyes of the world?"

" Yes, yes !" and " Name ! name !" cried a
hundred voices ; whilst a pair of stentorian
lungs shouted, from the gallery at the extreme
end of the room, " Why the deuce don't you
do it ? "

In the midst of the hubbub a grave, pale-faced
gentleman rose and said this kind of discussion
had gone far enough. He wanted to know the
exact position of the bank.

" Hear, hear ! " shouted several shareholders
close by ; whilst others could not help laughing
at this bit of clerical impracticability, seeing that
the report stated the position of the bank, and
the chairman's address had been furthermore
elucidatory.

The chairman rose to order, and was greeted
with cries of " Sit down ! " " Don't interfere ! "
" Let us have the name ! "

Meanwhile the financial orator stood, paper in
hand, calmly contemplating the scene, and half-
a-dozen other persons rose to speak, including the
poor parson, who had been induced to invest all

his money in this bank, chiefly on account of its classical connection with the East.

" I insist upon knowing the position of the bank," said the reverend gentleman, but his earnestness only raised a loud laugh.

" I fail to see the humorous side of my question," said the poor man, thinking of his wife and four little ones at the small rectory in Yorkshire. " Is this bank solvent, or is it not ? Is it going to break ? What is its position ? "

Laughter, cheers, and cries of " Bosh ! " and " Go on with the meeting ! " soon induced the poor rector to sit down, and then the financial orator said he would resume the case at the point where he had been interrupted.

" Name ! name ! " the shareholders cried, and several directors at length grew sufficiently excited to join in the chorus; but the financial orator begged to be permitted to explain the whole case before complying with the general request; and whilst he is gradually " piling up the agony," and drifting into his telling peroration, we propose to conduct you to an adjacent police court, where another extraordinary scene is being enacted.

We can return and pick up the "name" which the honorable proprietor has been asked for so frequently.

CHAPTER XVII.

CHIEFLY CONCERNS THE FORTUNES OF PAUL SOMERTON.

WHILST the honorable proprietor of the Eastern Bank was fulminating his financial thunders against somebody at present unnamed, Paul Somerton stood at the dock of a London police court.

The prisoner seemed to be overwhelmed with the degradation of his position.

The police inspector, who stood forward when the case was called from the charge sheet, said the prisoner had only been apprehended that morning. The evidence, however, was very short, and he thought it would hardly be necessary for him to ask for an adjournment. The prisoner was charged with stealing a purse containing three ten-pound notes, four sovereigns, and scrip of the Barwood Banking Company to the value of fifty pounds.

"Does anybody appear to watch the case for the prisoner?" asked the magistrate.

Nobody replied, and the magistrate, putting a gold-rimmed glass to his eye, addressed the prisoner.

"Judging from your dress and general appearance, you are respectably connected. Have you no friends here?"

"No, sir," said Paul. "But I am quite innocent of the charge which is made against me."

"Yes, prisoners mostly say so," said the magistrate, cynically; "but that must be inquired into."

"It is some horrible conspiracy, sir," said Paul with great earnestness, his lip quivering and his face quite pale with apprehension.

A gentleman who was sitting near the reporters rose at this juncture, and asked to be allowed to watch the case for the prisoner. Paul willingly embraced the offer on his part, and Mr. Arundel Williamson, a briefless barrister and a "gentleman of the press," stepped up to the prisoner, and entered into a brief conversation with Paul.

" Would you like the case to be adjourned for a short time ? " the magistrate asked.

"Thank you, no, sir," said Mr. Williamson ; and the police inspector called Mr. Shuffleton Gibbs, who stated that on the previous day he had business at the Meter Ironworks Company, Westminster. Whilst he was in Mr. Richard Tallant's room, he had occasion to take something from his purse, and during conversation he laid the purse upon the mantel-shelf. About half an hour afterwards, when he was leaving the room, he remembered his purse, and found that it was gone. At first he thought he must have put it into his pocket again, but he searched without avail. The only person who had come into the room whilst he was there was the prisoner.

" Will you ask Mr. Gibbs any questions, Mr. Williamson ? "

" No, sir, not at present," the barrister replied.

" Proceed with the case," said the magistrate.

Policeman X 40 said : " Late last night he had a search-warrant placed in his hands to execute at the house of Mr. Thomas Dibble, Still Street, Pimlico. He went there the next morning, and asked an old woman——"

" Old woman, thir !—how dare you call me an old woman ? " somebody exclaimed in the body of the police-court.

" Who is that ? Bring that woman forward," said the magistrate.

" Yeth, my lord and jury, or whatever you call yourthelveth," said Mrs. Dibble, elbowing herself, amidst much laughter, towards the bench.

" Silence !   Silence ! " exclaimed two police-men ; whilst another took hold of Mrs. Dibble's arm to increase her momentum.

" How dare you, thir ! Handth off, or I'll have the law againtht you for falthe imprithon-ment ; and ith more than your plathe ith worth to——"

"Take her out—take the woman out, if she will not be quiet," said the magistrate.

"At your peril," exclaimed Mrs. Dibble, amidst increasing laughter.

"Then out with her!" exclaimed the magistrate, losing his temper; and Mrs. Dibble speedily disappeared, struggling between two policemen, and bursting her hooks-and-eyes in the most extraordinary fashion.

"I asked the woman of the house," went on the imperturbable policeman, "to show me Paul Somerton's bedroom. She took me upstairs, and pointed a room out to me which she said was his. I asked if the box beneath the dressing-table was Paul Somerton's, and she said it was. I broke it open, and found at the bottom, beneath some clothes, the purse now produced. I then went to the offices of the Meter Ironworks and apprehended the prisoner."

"Is this your purse, Mr. Gibbs?" the magistrate inquired.

"It is," was that gentleman's reply.

"And the contents now are the same as when you lost it?"

"They are, sir," said Mr. Gibbs.

"Have you any questions to ask the policeman?" the magistrate inquired, addressing Mr. Williamson.

The barrister, after a short conversation with the prisoner, said he had not.

The police Inspector who had charge of the case asked if it would be necessary to call Mrs. Dibble to prove the ownership of the box wherein the purse was found.

Mr. Williamson said he thought, before the Court went any further with the case, it was well that he should apply for an adjournment until the next day. From the instructions of his client, who was, as the bench had judged, most respectably connected, he had no hesitation in saying that the case would turn out to be one of conspiracy against the prisoner; but he was hardly in a position to deal with it at so short a notice.

"At present there is ample evidence for committal to the sessions—a sufficiently *primâ facie* case for trial," said the magistrate. "Would it not be better to defer your defence until then?"

Mr. Williamson differed with the learned magistrate, and pressed for adjournment.

"Without bail, of course," said the magistrate.

"I think I shall be in a position to offer substantial bail in the course of an hour," said Paul's new friend.

"I shall be here for two hours," said the magistrate, "and will consider your application. I do not think I should be inclined to accept bail."

The prisoner was then removed, and his legal and journalistic friend went with him.

Mr. Williamson was a gentleman well known on the London press, not only for a certain cleverness in the epistolary style of writing, but for his peculiar amiability. Educated for the Church, certain scruples of conscience had induced him to give up the Establishment just when he was expected to be ready for ordination.

Afterwards he read for the Bar, was called in due time, and took up his quarters in the Temple. No briefs coming into his hands, he directed his attention to the Press, secured an appointment as critic on the *Sunday Review*, and was appointed London correspondent of *Berrow's Journal*, an old provincial paper of considerable repute. He joined the Hamilton Club, where Press-men most do congregate, and by degrees came to be regarded as one of the craft.

He was in the police-court during Paul's trouble quite by accident, having called in, out of kindness to little Simpkins, who was the accredited reporter of the *Daily Mercury*, and who was in a delicate state of health.

"I knew the little fellow was ill, and as he's only just pushing his way on the Press, I have dropped in occasionally and relieved him. His father was an old friend of my father's, and I feel a good deal of interest in him."

This was the brief explanation of Mr. Williamson's presence in court, which he thought it
necessary to give Paul, and then he sat down
quietly beside the prisoner, and made notes of all
that Paul wished him to know.

CHAPTER XVIII.

THE honourable proprietor continued to keep back his secret for some time, in face of all opposition ; several directors drew various devices on the blotting pads before them ; the reporters for the London papers smiled, took notes, sharpened their pencils, and nibbed their pens ; the Yorkshire cleric insisted upon knowing the position of the bank, and the stalwart layman from the same county loudly proclaimed his opinion that it was just simply "dommed nonsense to go on like this."

The financial orator was a gentleman of experience ; he had fought shareholders and directors before now, and he was not going to give way to these Eastern Bank fellows : he said this in a quiet whisper to a friendly M.P. who was standing by his side. Then turning towards the directorial seats, he said that a certain empty chair at the board that day did not at all surprise him.

"Name! name!" cried a few shareholders again; and then suddenly, for the first time, the chairman looked round the room nervously, as if he sought an absent face; and the shareholders gradually became quiet.

"The gentleman who is most conspicuous by his absence on this occasion is the absentee to whom I refer," said the financial orator.

Still the shareholders were at fault; some shook their heads, others looked as if they knew all about it; and the poor parson, in a moment of exhausted patience, again insisted upon knowing the position of the bank.

The chairman fidgetted uneasily in his seat: sundry anonymous letters making grave charges against his son, several questionable monetary transactions in which he had reason to suspect he was engaged, and one or two recent little disputes which he had had with his son, occurred to him, and he began to fear that the disclosure of the absentee's name would be a very painful one to himself.

At length the financial orator, after raising his hand for silence, said deliberately, "the gentleman to whom I refer is Mr. Richard Tallant;" and then there went a whisper all about the room— "The chairman's son!" In the public mind the name of Tallant had been so generally associated with everything that was honourable and true until now, that it seemed as if the bank was really broken indeed. London men looked silently and inquiringly at each other. Country shareholders, who had never previously attended these half-yearly meetings, looked on in amazement, and wondered what would be the next turn in the mysterious wheel of fortune.

All this occurred in much less time than it occupies you to read what we have written by way of narrative. Not many moments elapsed before the chairman rose. He beckoned the speaker who had denounced his son, and the gentleman came up and began expressing regret at being compelled to take a course which must be so painful to the chairman.

"Nay, nay, make no apologies, sir; you have simply discharged your duty," said Mr. Tallant. "What proofs have you?"

The honourable proprietor handed to the chairman a bundle of papers. Having carefully examined these through his eye-glass, and apologised for detaining the meeting, Mr. Tallant, in a voice which fully indicated the mental agony of the speaker, said—"Gentlemen, you will readily understand what a blow this is to me. When I rose to order it was not for a moment with any idea of screening my son——"

"Query," said a wretched shareholder, who was hissed, and hustled, too, in a moment.

"It has been my pride," said the chairman, heedless of the interruption, "throughout my long business career, to make the name of Tallant one of strength in this great metropolis, and a name

which should be synonymous with wealth and
with honour. My ambition was unbounded, you
may say, but surely it was a laudable ambition.
I say surely it was, more now by way of question
than by way of assertion; perhaps the standard
which I set up was too high. But until to-day
I seem to have reached the acme of all my pride
and hope; for never before, I believe, has a word
been even whispered against the honour, and
integrity, and soundness of a Tallant."

Cries of "Hear, hear!" and a weak attempt at
cheering, greeted the fine old man, as he looked
round the room with something like an air of
triumph in his misery.

"I have held a high place amongst you now
for many years; but we have fallen upon bad
times. We are in the midst of a financial crisis
which is not only breaking banks but friendships;
which is not only carrying wreck and ruin to the
weak and the false, the fool and the knave, but
which is shaking the reputations of men of pro-
bity and honour. The suggestion of an honourable

proprietor, made this day, that I should resign, was greeted with a sufficient sound of approving voices to determine me in my course, before this attack upon my son. It had been my full intention to resign (cries of "No, no!" and "Yes, yes!") I have no other alternative."

Here the cries of "No, no!" and "Yes, yes!" broke out afresh, and somebody said, "How do we know he isn't as bad as his son?"

When something like quiet was once more restored, Mr. Tallant said, "I have been your chairman now for nearly five years. I have striven to do my duty to this great corporation. Through misfortunes over which the directors could have but little control, the failure of some great houses in Bombay——"

"And your own mismanagement," said a fierce and irrepressible shareholder, who had five thousand pounds locked up in the concern, and who thought this a sufficient warrant for being angry and insolent.

But Mr. Tallant did not appear to hear these

galling remarks, howsoever deeply they may have impressed him.

"And through the failure of some great houses in Bombay," he repeated, "our Indian branches have suffered a loss of one hundred thousand pounds."

Loud groans, and other expressions of anger and contempt, greeted this announcement. In the midst of it the chairman, who had taken a cheque-book from his pocket, sat down, and with a trembling hand filled it up, and signed it with his well-known clear bold signature.

Raising his hand to command silence, he said, "One hundred thousand pounds represents your losses by these failures—the only losses this corporation have suffered during my presidency. Here is a cheque for the amount, and I shall—never—occupy this chair again."

Mr. Tallant deliberately handed the cheque to the secretary of the company, who sat near him, and taking up his hat proceeded to leave the room. The shareholders and others made way for the fine old English gentleman as he passed, and in a few moments his firm steady footstep could be heard on the staircase.

Some minutes elapsed before it occurred to several friends that they ought to follow him. By the time they reached the street Mr. Tallant was nowhere to be seen. He had called a hansom, and ordered the driver to go to the Paddington Railway Station : and he sat there in the waiting-room for nearly an hour. Trains came and went whilst he sat there; people came in and out, happy mothers and children, merry West-coun-trymen, and London tourists, and sorrowful-looking people also.

The sunlight was struggling through the great glass roof of the station, and making the place look quite joyful and festive. White wreaths of steam from noisy engines crept up to the glass, and dispersed in a sparkling kind of mist. There was a general air of pleasantness about the place that was cheering; but the great London mer-chant sat in the waiting-room with his arms folded, and his head upon his breast, waiting for the train.

You have stood at a railway station and seen them shunting a train of carriages upon some weed-grown siding. It seemed as if Fate had shunted the owner of Barton Hall—as if his day were over, as if, after going bravely through the world for a long time, he had broken down, and had come to be shunted upon a siding. Not shunted, like you and we hope to be shunted some day, smoothly and quietly to rest from our labours ; but roughly, ruthlessly, thrust and bumped into a line of off-rails, covered with the dust of the world, and ticketed "Not to be used."

It was a bitterly hard lot for Christopher Tallant, in his prime and in his glory, but he knuckled down to it manfully, and bent his head to the storm.

The train came at last, and carried the merchant away to the station nearest Barton Hall. The porters were in a state of great excitement because there was no carriage as usual to meet

Mr. Tallant; he took no notice of their inquiries and suggestions beyond the courtesy of a passing nod, but walked quietly to the principal hotel. Thence he sent a messenger requesting a local lawyer to attend him at Barton Hall, whither he departed as quickly as a hired conveyance would permit.

They had heard of the panic at this little out-of-the-way town, and concluded at once that Mr. Tallant had received some great financial injury in the crisis. The town was alive with rumours all the night, and by bed-time Mr. Tallant was reported to have lost a million of money in railways. But on the following day the true story was told by the London papers, or by one of them at least; for the majority had excluded the point of the denunciatory speech which ended with the name of Richard Tallant.

The law of libel, as it affects newspaper proprietors, is peculiar with regard to the publication of public sayings and doings. The reporter may set down the most scurrilous and libellous speech which counsel or solicitor may make in a court of justice, and the newspaper editor may publish it in his columns without a shadow of legal responsibility resting upon him; but anything said at a public meeting which in any way affects the character or reputation of a private individual or a public man, is published at the editor's peril: so that several of the London journals refrained from chronicling all that took place at the Eastern Bank meeting. One editor, bolder than the rest, published the meeting at length; and his paper it was which enlightened the people in the Avonworth Valley with regard to the unusual manner and conduct of the famous proprietor of Barton Hall.

CHAPTER XIX.

OF CERTAIN REPORTS IN THE NEWSPAPERS.

O, THOSE hard and bitter histories, the newspapers! Hard as the metal in which they are
printed. Stern matter-of-fact histories of the
great world. They go straight to the subject;
they do not prepare the reader by any quiet pre-
liminary caution that the man who has been
found murdered is his father; there is nothing
roundabout in that long list of deaths. You have
no time to think before the awful truth is in
your mind. That railway accident,—is your dear
friend unhurt?—whilst you are wondering, there
stands his name in the list of dead. That little
indiscretion of your son's;—here it is, blazoned
forth to the world in the police reports: he was
only anxious to save his friend, and his zeal over-

came his discretion; he is fined for obstructing a policeman in the execution of his duty, and here stands the record, to be turned against him any-day.

O, hard and bitter histories! They told the story on that second day. They told the two stories. They came to Barton Hall, wrapped up carefully and smug as of yore. They were carried to the kitchen fire and dried. John scanned them, and saw nothing of importance. Mary noticed a frightful murder stuck down in one corner, almost out of sight. Peter the groom took note of the latest betting; but none of them saw what the people at the town found out later in the day; and none of them saw what Phœbe Tallant and Amy Somerton saw.

Mr. Tallant had been engaged until late with his country lawyer, and had kept his room on that second day. Phœbe was sure there was something seriously the matter with her father; for he had pressed her hand, and kissed her, and made the tears come into her eyes.

This was something very unusual for Mr. Tallant. Proud as he undoubtedly was of Phœbe's beauty, hers was a sort of negative existence in his mind. Richard, her brother, had engrossed nearly all his thoughts. Phœbe was like a simple flower adorning the name of Tallant;—but Richard, he would build up the house and perpetuate the name, and be the grand, educated successor of his father.

Once or twice, however, within the few previous months, grave doubts as to the propriety of his son's conduct had crossed the merchant's mind; but these had been to a great extent dispelled by a few words of conversation with his son. Of course, the young fellow had been educated at Oxford, and had thoughts, and feelings, and aspirations altogether different to his father's. The old man understood this to a certain extent, but " honour, Dick; remember, that does not come with college education, my boy," Mr. Tallant would say; " don't let Latin, and Greek, and mythology, and grand acquaintances shake plain old Saxon notions of honour and honesty, and paying your way, and owing no man, and all those old-fashioned things which have made the name of Tallant foremost in the city of London."

But Richard Tallant was in the whirlpool of fast life, of speculation, of financial scheming, of gambling; and at length he reached the vortex, with all the good lessons and examples of his father upon his head.

So these newspapers, as we have said, were dried, and whilst a couple were sent up-stairs to Mr. Tallant, two were taken into the drawing-room to Miss Tallant and her friend, Miss Somerton.

Never did papers contain so much to startle and interest two girls before. The Eastern Bank meeting, and the exposure of Richard Tallant; the charge of robbery against Paul Somerton; and a paragraph recording the departure of the troop-ship *Atlas* for India, with Captain the Hon. Lionel Hammerton on board.

They mastered it all at last, and clung to each other in terror and amazement. It seemed almost as if the world had suddenly come to an end. Phœbe looked round, as if to assure herself that she was at home. There was no mistaking this. The familiar chairs and cabinets, and pictures and statuettes, all seemed to look reassuringly at her.

Amy took things in a more demonstrative fashion. She pressed her hand to her head, and then broke forth into a low wail of pain.

"And I did not know that he even intended to leave the country," said Amy, by-and-by, all her thoughts concentrated upon Lionel Hammerton.

Phœbe, with her brother's disgrace, her father's misery, and Paul Somerton's troubles, each agitating her mind in turns, had scarcely thought for a moment of the sudden and unexplained departure of Lionel Hammerton. Arthur Phillips might have told her of it, but the artist had not been near Barton Hall for more than a month. He had written a note of apology, and explaining that his absence was necessary for the completion of some important work upon which he was engaged.

"Not even to say good-bye," Amy exclaimed, rocking herself to and fro.

It quite shocked Phœbe to see how Amy dwelt upon this departure of Hammerton; to see how it overshadowed all the other bitter news. Amy had not even uttered one expression of pity for the brother whom she loved so well.

This secret love of Lionel Hammerton had burned itself into her very nature. However much she might have doubted her powers to bring him to her side, and however much she may have despaired of the return of her love, on the ground of their great disparity of position, she had long since been convinced that Lionel cared a little for her. She had brooded over his acts of kindness and courtesy; she had bound up his image in all her ways of life, and Phœbe knew how much she loved him.

His leaving without explanation, and without a

word at parting, was not only a blow to the girl's soft and tender dreams of love returned, but it struck at her pride, and brought her down to the abject thing at which she had seemed to rate herself in her thoughts of the greatness and glory of Lionel Hammerton.

There might have been something like the aping of humility in this girl's love; in her own estimation she had been as nothing compared with him, to whom she had given up her secret soul; but, trodden upon and slighted, she rose up, conscious of her own beauty, and with a sense of her own deserts, burning with wounded pride.

" He treats me with contempt and indifference, Phœbe," she said, casting the newspaper upon the floor, and trampling upon it. "Let him; he shall have scorn for scorn, contempt for contempt. Does he think that a woman's heart is to be trampled upon because of lowly birth? Does he think true love and English chivalry have exclusive inheritance amongst the titled and the wealthy? Does he think I am a poor silly country girl, with a weak, pliable nature, that will bend and adapt itself to whatever may turn up in a jog-trot country life? He shall see; he shall see."

With this Amy Somerton swept out of the room like an enraged queen, who counted her subjects by millions.

"Poor Amy, she has read too much poetry of late, and thought it all true," said Phœbe, the big tears rolling down her fair cheek. "Whatever will become of us all! I am sure my head swims with the thought of all the dreadful things that have taken place. My poor dear father!" then she exclaimed, and the next minute she had burst into his room, and flung herself upon his neck.

"Dear, dear father," she said, "do bear up; perhaps it is not true; perhaps he has repented, and all may come right again," said Phœbe, smoothing the merchant's grey hair; but she felt how hopeless was Richard's case notwithstanding.

Mr. Tallant submitted to his daughter's ca-
resses, and his mind was suddenly carried back to
the days of his second wife. In the midst of
great trouble and distress of mind the thoughts
will often ramble to times and things altogether
apart from the immediate cause of your mental
anxiety. Mr. Tallant thought of the wife whom
he had loved so dearly, and then wondered that
no likeness remained of her in his child.

"You are not quite ruined, perhaps, father,"
said the girl, by-and-by; "we can go and live in
some quiet little place, where we shall be
unknown."

"Ruined, my love," said the merchant, with a
faint smile, "what made you think of that?"

"That great sum of money which you paid,
father—so nobly, so like your true self," said the
girl, with a look of admiration shining through
her tears.

"I could do that several times over, and be far
from ruined then," said the merchant, with just a
touch of pride in his manner; "it is our name

that is ruined, our name that is blemished; *his* name—he who was to be the pride of the land."

"But the paper says the name of Tallant has risen higher than ever with your magnanimous and noble revenge," said Phœbe, timidly, for she had never in all her life before spoken to her father of money and things appertaining to trade and commerce.

"The papers!" repeated the merchant, bitterly. "What can they say or do? Who cares for the papers in times like these, when the greatest houses in the country are tottering to their very foundation. The name of Tallant would have risen like a rock of gold in this panic, and been impressed for all time in the history of finance, but for this wretched, this miserable deception."

"But your own name, father; your own honour," said the girl.

"What do I care for myself," said the merchant, interrupting her; "it was for him that I worked, and saved, and hoarded. Did I grudge him? No; he was his own master; he had the run of my own bank. But there, there, Phœbe, say no more upon the subject. We will try to talk of other things."

"The Somertons, too, will be in great distress," said Phœbe, "about their son."

"Why?" asked the merchant.

"Did you not read it in the paper?"

"I have read nothing in the paper," was the reply.

"In prison, and charged with robbery," said Phœbe, softly; "but a counsel appeared for him and said it was a conspiracy."

"That is easily said," the merchant answered. "Robbery! whom has *he* robbed?"

Phœbe shuddered at the emphasis in the latter sentence, which convinced her that her father's opinion of Richard was sealed and settled.

"His prosecutor is a person named Gibbs— Shuffleton Gibbs," said Phœbe.

"The greatest scoundrel in London," said the

merchant. " Better to have such a man against you than for you ; he is the intimate and bosom friend of your brother. Give me the paper, love, and leave me to read it."

Phœbe opened out the paper which lay upon the table, kissed her father's forehead, and went to comfort the Somertons.

She looked the very impersonation of comfort and consolation, this gentle, confiding, Miranda-like being, as she quietly glided across the park towards the farm. An old shepherd dog came bounding up to her, and leaping for joy, in its half-blind, shambling fashion ; a little group of deer trotted off before her, but turned round to look, and said as plainly as could be, " We should not have moved, had it not been for that villainous dog ;" ducks, and hens, and chickens, all came round about her as she entered the farm enclosure ; a great furry cat came and purred beside her ; and Mr. Somerton's blackbird, which hung by the window in a wicker cage, began to sing so merrily that you could hardly hear the whirr and rattle of the threshing-machine, which was hard at work in the adjacent stack-yard.

Whilst Amy Somerton was pacing to and fro in her chamber at the Hall, Phœbe Tallant fulfilled her office at the Hall Farm, and endeavoured in a hundred gentle, gracious ways to console the bailiff and his wife. So far as Luke was concerned, she was not unsuccessful, but Mrs. Somerton gave way to her feelings without the slightest regard to Amy's consolatory observations.

The farmer's wife seemed to arraign all humanity as if it were in a conspiracy against her, and she was almost rude to Miss Tallant, so much so that Luke interposed in an authoritative manner, and Phœbe looked hurt and concerned.

This only changed the manner of Mrs. Somerton's complainings. She was satisfied that Paul was guilty. He must have stolen the purse; it didn't often happen, she went on, that people got charged with offences of that kind unless they deserved it. All her children went wrong; none of them cared for her; none of them made any return to her for all her care.

Nobody knew her trials, nobody could understand her troubles; all she hoped was, that the time would come soon, when they would be ended for ever.

Luke Somerton rated his wife in a quiet, manly fashion for her injustice towards Paul, and her unkind return for the generous attention of Miss Tallant; and by-and-by Mrs. Somerton began to cry, and that was a sufficient apology to the rich merchant's daughter, who sat beside the bailiff's wife and said all sorts of comforting things, whilst Mr. Somerton set about packing up a carpet-bag for the purpose of going to London; and eventually Miss Somerton presented herself, and requested that she might be permitted to accompany her father.

CHAPTER XX.

' IN this world the victory is not always with the good and the true. It has shaken many a man's faith before now to see the wicked and the selfish thrive, whilst the noble, and the generous, and the pure, were beggars.

Suppose there were no hereafter? What would compensate us for the unequal justice which, judged by the world's standard, is meted out? What would hinder the unfortunate and poverty-stricken from making their quietus with a bare bodkin? What would reconcile the man bound to work on, and toil on, and sweat and drudge in misery, from eating his very life out with envy of the rich? What would prevent the wealthy man who, willing to help his poorer brethren to the fullest extent, finds individual help like his of comparatively little use—what would there be left for him but to put down the unequal distribution of riches to gross injustice? How could we reconcile it with a good and beneficent Creator, that some are born and bred in poverty and wretchedness, and are doomed to wear the chain of want all their lives; whilst others inherit all the luxuries of purple and fine linen, and chairs of state and command? What else but a future of rewards and punishments would enable us to live and endure all this, rich and poor, good and bad, selfish and generous?

Honesty is the best policy in the end, so far as personal happiness is concerned. It is a selfish way of preaching honesty nevertheless; but how often, in a worldly sense, does the axiom seem to be reversed. On the Stock Exchange there were certain men who were dishonest. They lied wilfully and designedly about the credit of banks

and companies; they propagated scandalous reports about certain establishments; they sent
out thousands of lying letters throughout the
country, cautioning people against concerns which
they knew to be safe. Then they went into the
market and sold shares which they did not
possess, and secured low quotations in the newspapers. This frightened people who had invested
their money honourably, and they began to sell.
Confidence was shaken, and the "bears" made
money. Their lies and dishonesty ruined hundreds of honest people; but men like young
Tallant and Mr. Gibbs profited by the transactions. They bought and sold at pleasure, and
in the midst of the general panic selected what
concern they liked for ruin.

It is true that by degrees the gentlemen known
as "bears" created a storm which they could not
control, and that some fell by their own thunder
—some were caught in their own snares; whilst
others thrived and waxed rich, and retired on
handsome fortunes, many of them made by pur-

chasing at a low figure shares which they had assisted to depreciate.

Young Tallant was amongst those who made large sums of money. He was fortunate in all he undertook ; and on that very morning when he was denounced at the great City meeting, his "bearing" speculations represented a profit to the tune of many thousands. It was in this wise : he was a director of the Mercantile Finance Bank. On the previous day the shares had been run down by false reports to ten shillings a share— scrip upon which twenty pounds had been paid. Young Tallant bought two thousand shares at the close of the market. The next day the *Times* contradicted the rumours, the directors made a statement, confidence was restored in a few hours, and the director who knew that such would be the case, sold his two thousand at an average of more than seven pounds a share.

Since the row at the Ashford Club he had acted more upon his own account, and had avoided Mr. Shuffleton Gibbs, who, left to his own machinations, had been a little too clever in his stock-jobbing operations; he had sold largely shares which had rallied, and were likely to stand all future assaults. But he still had schemes on hand which seemed likely to bear substantial monetary fruits. He was rich enough, as the readers of this history will no doubt have guessed, to encompass his revenge against Paul Somerton.

The plot had been well and skilfully managed. Thomas Dibble had led a life of dreadful misery since his loss of the five hundred pounds, and Mr. Gibbs had aggravated his torture with a thumb-screwish perfection of cruelty. The shares which Thomas Dibble had bought carried a future responsibility of fifteen hundred pounds. So that his loss, instead of being five hundred, might really have been increased to two thousand.

Mr. Gibbs, by degrees, explained this to the wretched Dibble, who had lain awake during long weary nights, beside the partner of his bosom, suffering all sorts of agonies, and without daring to explain his misery to Mrs. D., who said enough every day and night about the five hundred pounds to have broken down more sensitive minds than Dibble's.

"I do really think I shall go mad," he said to Mr. Gibbs, on the day when that gentleman had tortured him up to the last pitch necessary for making Dibble his tool.

"Then I must save you," said Mr. Gibbs, at length.

"Oh, Mr. Gibbs, dont 'e trifle with my feelings," said Thomas.

"Not I, my friend; I intended to have assisted you when I advised you to buy those shares, and I am sorry they have not turned out so well as we had a right to expect," said Mr. Gibbs, tapping his tight little boots with a cane, and looking up at the lamp under which Dibble had accosted him in the street.

"No, no—the best intentions sir; but dear, dear, bad be the best this time."

"Come to my chambers in an hour, Dibble, and I will see if I can put the thing right."

"Yes, sir," said Dibble, touching his cap; the two parted, and in an hour Dibble was sitting on the edge of a chair in Mr. Gibbs' private room.

"Business is business," said Mr. Gibbs; "I will take the shares from you, and here is a cheque for five hundred pounds."

"God bless 'e, God bless 'e !" began Dibble, in an ecstasy of delight.

"Stop a little; there is a small condition," said Mr. Gibbs, placing his hand upon a purse which he laid upon the table.

Dibble looked at Mr. Gibbs for explanation, but quite prepared in his own mind to buy peace at home at any sacrifice.

"You must put this purse secretly into Paul Somerton's box, in his bedroom."

Dibble looked puzzled, and Gibbs fixed him with his fishy eye.

"It is a very simple thing. Take it without

examination, and find an opportunity to-night to put it carefully in the lowest corner, underneath his clothes or papers, or whatever else he has in his box."

"Yes, it be simple," said Dibble, patting his forehead, and looking at his boots; "it be very simple, that's true."

"Do it, and to-morrow morning give me your shares and I give you five hundred pounds; here is one hundred on account to-night, in proof of my sincerity."

"Oh, that be all right, sir—I can trust to what you says; but what be the meaning of this business about the purse?"

"I like your question—nothing like being open and straightforward with each other. That's my motto," said Gibbs.

"And it be a good un, too," said Thomas.

"Paul Somerton has done me a serious injury, and I am determined to punish him; he is a conceited, proud young fellow, and I mean to take him down."

"He be proud, that's true," said Dibble, re-membering how Paul had dropped his companion-ship of late.

"I hate and detest him, he is a thief and a scoundrel; and I could have him transported if I liked."

"Could you now?" said Dibble, staring in amazement at Mr. Gibbs, who, despite his efforts to appear calm, had clenched his fist, and looked particularly ugly.

"I shall punish him by means of this purse. If you do what I require you will have your five hundred pounds, and have no liability beyond it; and you will be able to live comfortably and happily again with Mrs. Dibble. And if you don't, you will have fifteen hundred pounds to pay beyond the five hundred; you will be sold up and turned out of house and home, and be done up root and branch."

Dibble groaned aloud at this picture, and jumping from his seat, said, "Give me the purse, give it me; I'll do it."

"And you swear on your oath—go down on your knees—there, that will do; now you swear that whatever may take place you will never confess that you know anything about the purse, or ever saw it in your life before."

"I swear it all," said Dibble.

"So help you, heaven!" said Gibbs, holding his hand aloft, and Dibble repeated the imprecation.

"If you should break your oath you will not only go to the devil," said Gibbs, solemnly, "but you will before that be taken by the police as a thief, and transported. Now, here are ten ten-pound notes, and here is the purse; in the morning early I shall know if you have done your work properly. Good night."

"Good night," said Dibble, slinking away in a perspiration of fear and happiness, of doubt and hope; afraid of his own shadow, yet less afraid of Mrs. Dibble than he had been a few hours before.

And this is how the purse came to be in Paul Somerton's box; and this is how it was that Mrs. Dibble's joy at seeing her five hundred pounds on the table before her was neutralised by Paul Somerton's apprehension, and the insulting manner of the policeman towards both herself and her establishment.

That night of Paul's apprehension and remand was a terrible one for poor Dibble.; for during the evening there arrived Paul's father and sister Amy, and he was witness of their distress and trouble. He sat there and listened to Amy's stories of his goodness, and he saw the silent sorrow of his fine manly father. He heard Mrs. Dibble speak of Paul as the best and kindest young man; and he felt that she was speaking nothing but the truth when she said she would rather have lost a thousand pounds than such a thing should have happened.

And by-and-by Mr. Williamson, the barrister who had spoken up for Paul, came to the house in a cab, bringing Paul with him; which was such a blow to Dibble that he had not the heart to join in the general expressions of delight at the poor young fellow's appearance. He sat there looking on, so pale and woe-begone, that Mrs. Dibble was struck with his appearance, and pitied him for taking the thing so much to heart.

There was quite a scene between Amy and Paul, neither of them expecting to see each other. Amy rushed into his arms and sobbed on his shoulder, until Paul could hardly help crying himself; and Mrs. Dibble burst every hook-and-eye she had left. And Dibble could stand it no longer; so he slunk away into the back kitchen, with serious thoughts of putting his head into the water-butt, and keeping it there until he was dead. After five minutes' consideration he changed his mind, and returned to the little parlour calmer and more contented, and sufficiently at ease to shake hands with the released prisoner, for whom Mr. Williamson had succeeded in giving bail.

CHAPTER XXI.

WHEREIN THOMAS DIBBLE "RUNS AWAY," AND
MEETS WITH A VERY REMARKABLE COMPANION.

MRS. DIBBLE insisted upon Miss Somerton and
her father remaining in her house until the next
day, when Paul was to reappear at Bow Street;
and this increase in the Dibbleonian establishment
made it necessary that Mr. Thomas Dibble should
sleep on the sofa in the parlour.

"I'll make you up a comfortable bed, Thomath,"
said Mrs. D., when all the other members of the
household had retired to rest, "particularly on
account of your sympathy with that young man;
for if ever there was innocence anywhere it is in
his face: though however that purse could get into
his box is a matter as I have yet to learn. It's very
well for Mr. Williamson, that barrister gentleman—

who reminds me of a young man as made me an offer before I left boarding-school, which my parenth were particular in sending me to on account of the position I was expected to take in the world— and he may say it with perfect truth, that some one has got into the house and put that purse into his box; but how to get the police to believe it is another thing : but we shall see in the morning."

"They'll believe it, Maria," said Thomas, very solemnly, with his eyes fixed upon his wife's buxom figure, which would obtrude its plumpness and its whiteness through her tight dresses, either in front or behind, and more particularly in an evening when Mrs. Dibble unbuttoned her dress for the purpose of being able to breathe more freely.

"They will ?—it's all very well to say they will, but if Mr. Williamson can do no more than show the animas, as he calls it, of the persecutor Mr. Gibbs, it strikes me—judging from the villainous manner of those policeman, who will not allow anyone else to speak except themselves—that Mr. Williamson will only waste his breath."

And Mrs. Dibble went on laying sheets and blankets between a sofa and three chairs, and tucking them down at the foot and making the two pillows go as far as possible in height by the aid of the sofa cushions and an old carpet bag; whilst Dibble looked on very sadly, but calmly, and wondered what Mrs. Dibble would think in the morning when she entered the room and found that the extempore bed had never been used.

"Will you give me a kiss before you go to bed, Maria?" said Dibble, in an appealing tone.

"Of course I will, Thomath; for the way as you snatched that five hundred pounds out of the fire, as I may say, deserves ever so many kisses, Thomath, and as done everything to make our lives happy again, though, as I have said before, it was not the money so much as deceiving me, Thomath; I did think I never could have forgiven that; but there, it's all over, Thomath, and seeing other people in trouble makes one's heart softer than usual: and so bless you, Thomath, bless you."

Whereupon Mrs. Dibble put her arms round poor Dibble's neck and bade him good-night.

"And good-bye!" said Dibble, when she was going up-stairs; "And good-bye, Maria!" he repeated when he heard the door shut upon her. For Thomas Dibble when he went out into the back kitchen and contemplated the water-butt, determined to run away. Not only to run away, but to leave behind him a confession of the part he had taken in the conspiracy against Paul Somerton.

He sat down before the handful of smouldering cinders in the little parlour grate, and thought out his plan. He had suffered much from Mrs. Dibble about the five hundred pounds; he had purchased peace by its return, and she had forgiven him. But how had he bought peace? If he remained where he was, he would be sure to confess, and then what would Maria say? what would Paul say? what would his sister say? what did his own conscience say now? He could not endure the latter, even in secret, and how could he bear the former?

No, he would run away. His master was at home, in grief and sorrow for the disgrace of his son. That son had dishonoured the name of Tallant, and Paul Somerton was on the verge of becoming an outcast. It would be better that he, Thomas Dibble, should go forth and become a wanderer and a beggar than that the innocent should suffer, and bring disgrace upon a respectable family.

Then poor old Dibble thought about his oath, and fear came upon him in a remembrance of the dreadful consequences which Mr. Gibbs had described. Then he thought of Maria, but a bitter memory of the wretched life he had led with her, during the monetary interregnum, steeled him slightly against her, and he consoled himself with the feeling that at least she had the money back again.

A hundred other things occurred to Thomas as

reasons why he should run away, and why he should not. It was dishonourable to take an oath and take a man's money without sticking to the bargain; but no gentleman ought to have inveigled a poor man into such a plot. No matter which way Thomas looked at the case, he saw himself a disgraced man; but he thought there was far less disgrace in running away than in staying behind, and a thousand times more disgrace in letting the affair go on than in preventing the conspiracy from taking effect.

So Thomas decided that he would go, that he would be a wanderer, a beggar, a tramp,—anything but a persecutor of the innocent. He would eat Mrs. Dibble's bread-and-butter no longer.

It occupied him nearly two hours to write out in his big, round, straggling hand a brief account of his share in the plot to ruin Paul, and having done this, and signed it, and laid it in the middle of the parlour table, directed to Paul Somerton, he wrote on another sheet of paper, "Farwell,

Maria, and if for ever, may you forgiv your herring sinner, T. Dibble."

Then the model porter of the Meter Works thought it would be only fair to let Mr. Gibbs know that he had confessed all. He, therefore, wrote a very short but very large letter to "Mr. Shuffleton Gibbs, Esq.," determining to leave London by the West End, and put the letter under the door of Mr. Gibbs' lodgings as he passed by.

It was on a fine, bright, starlight autumn morning that Thomas Dibble went forth on his pilgrimage.

Turning out of his way a little he pushed the letter under Mr. Gibbs' door, and then directed his steps towards Paddington. He preferred to take the longest way through the streets, because he thought he would like to tread them once more, and say good-bye, as it were, to familiar scenes. On past Westminster he trudged, with a little bundle over his shoulder, on past the Houses of Parliament, where he encountered an early coffee man, and invested in an early cup of his refreshing beverage. He would fain have had a pennyworth of pudding, but the pudding men were all abed,.and so were the vendors of chesnuts. The police were awake, and Thomas chuckled quietly to himself, as he passed certain active members of the force, upon the way in which they would be sold at Bow Street next day.

He trudged on past Charing Cross and through the Haymarket, along Regent Street and past Regent's Circus, meeting a few roysterers, early workmen going to half-built houses, and printers going home from daily newspaper offices; he saw a few shambling tramps hanging about doorways, and seeking intervals of repose on doorsteps, whence they were ousted occasionally by policemen; he met stray cabs with early fares, scavengers, and slouching women reeling from infamous dens in by-streets; and he wondered when it would be daylight.

By-and-by the great city and its smiling suburbs

were left behind, and Thomas was on the white
highway, with hedges right and left, and market-
gardens behind them ; and then morning dawned,
and he journeyed on beside carts and waggons,
and met tramps with dusty boots and jackets ;
for the autumn had been a particularly dry
season, and the roads were covered with dust.

At length the afternoon began to wane, and
Dibble turned into the fields, over a stile, and sat
down beside some half-cut corn and untied his
bundle. A piece of bread and cheese dropped
out, and Thomas, being hungry, fell to with a will.
Whilst he was eating, a miserable, lean, lank-look-
ing dog came crouching and smelling towards
him. Alone in the wide world, Thomas naturally
felt some little sympathy with the vagrant dog,
and he threw it a piece of bread and then a piece
of cheese. The animal, making certain apologetic
snaps at the crumbs, ate them, and then stood
upon his hind-legs and seemed to beg for more.
Dibble could not help smiling at the quaint,
gaunt, spectral-looking dog, with all its ribs

showing through its tight ragged skin; and he fed it again. Then the animal walked round Dibble, on his hind legs, and performed a sort of double shuffle. Dibble was highly amused with this performance, and he laughed very heartily and patted the dog on the head. The animal wagged his tail, turned a somersault, and stood upon his head in such a comical fashion that poor Dibble fairly rolled on his back with laughing, the dog leaping over him and barking in the most extraordinary and un-doglike fashion.

Thus Thomas Dibble made friends with this singular animal, and resolved to have it as his travelling companion if his dogship would consent. The dog was nothing loth, and the companionship led to important results in the history of Thomas Dibble's adventures.

CHAPTER XXII.

IN WHICH THOMAS DIBBLE CONTINUES TO "RUN AWAY."

THIS strange, mongrel-looking dog, which Dibble encountered amongst the corn, was not only a source of amusement to the runaway porter, but gave rise to a variety of speculations far beyond the usual scope of Dibble's imagination.

As the evening came on, and the mist began to rise upon the brooks and rivers, and the leaves whirled about amongst the dust, however, poor Dibble's somewhat dull imagination took its hue from surrounding objects, and he suddenly became very thoughtful. He looked at the dog as it walked by his side, with its nose nearly upon the ground and its stumpy tail sticking up behind, and a sense of fear came over him.

All at once it occurred to Dibble that the devil could assume any shape he pleased. Supposing this dog were the devil, come to claim the price of the broken oath which Dibble had sworn to Gibbs! Just then the dog began to walk on his hind legs and barked, as if to confirm Dibble's supposition.

The runaway porter quickened his pace immediately, and his heart sunk within him. He was glad to see a cart coming along the road; this re-assured him, and he began to run as fast as he could; but the dog soon dropped on all fours again, and overtook his companion.

Dibble would have cried out to the carter for help, but just at that moment he came to a bend in the road, and saw a roadside inn and a little village not many yards ahead. The dog, it would seem, saw the inn, too, and the sight was not so pleasant to him as to Dibble, for the dog stood still, and then turned tail and crept into the hedge, and howled. Thomas was surprised at this, and plucked up courage enough to whistle and beckon his companion, believing that if the dog were not the devil, it was staying behind because of Dibble's unkindness in running away, and feeling that if it were the devil he might get some assistance in the village to kill him, and thus get rid of the devil for ever; which Thomas, in his own way, thought would be a grand achievement.

It was some little time before the dog acknowledged Dibble's sympathetic whistles and encouraging words to "come along;" but at length the vagrant animal came forth, and walked sadly and solemnly at the porter's heels.

They went into the roadside inn together, along the passage, past the bar window, and into the tap-room, where two or three rough-looking fellows were drinking beer. Dibble sat down, and the dog slunk away into a corner under a long seat with a high back, called a "settle." One of the men, a little fellow with a fur cap on his head, and a brown velvet jacket on his back, evidently noticed the dog, for he smiled and winked at another fellow, who sat opposite to him.

"There'll be some fun jest now," said the little man, looking at Dibble, who called for a pint of ale.

Several other people came in at this moment, three women amongst the rest. Most of them had bundles, and the men all wore caps and shabby coats ; the women wore shawls and showy ribbons, and spoke in a hoarse, foggy style, and reminded Dibble of the women he remembered presiding over nut-stalls and shooting galleries at the Gloucestershire fairs when he was a boy.

Whilst he was drinking his beer the window at the back was darkened with several show-houses, caravans, and ricketty canvas-covered carts, which were coming into the yard for the night, and then Dibble knew that he was amongst show people. He ventured to ask an old man, who sat next to him, and who was engaged in spinning a penny in a peculiar way, and twitching it up his sleeve, if there was a fair coming off.

"Severntown races," said the man, continuing his occupation, and evincing a desire not to be interrupted.

"Oh!" said Dibble, looking round, and taking stock of his new acquaintances. Several of them, he saw, had bundles like himself, and all of them produced something to eat. Bread and sausages, bread and herrings, bread and cheese, bread and onions, bread and black-pudding, bread and tripe; and bread and many other things were exhumed from those mysterious bundles, and from deep greasy pockets. The edibles were demolished along with beer, and gin-and-water, and porter, and cider, and other liquors, which a thick-fisted waiter brought in, amidst much talking and some swearing.

All this time the little man in the velvet coat kept careful watch over Dibble and the dog; and by-and-by, when the man who had been spinning the penny went out with a person in an overcoat and tights (who had been standing on his head in the villages through which he passed, and doing other funny tricks upon a square piece of carpet), the little man went and sat beside Dibble, at whom he nodded pleasantly, and for whose especial behoof he tapped a nose somewhat flattened by hard usage and dirty weather.

"I forgives yer, old gal, I forgives yer," he said, directing one eye towards the dog's hiding-place, and winking at Dibble with the other.

Whereupon the dog came forth, rubbed his bony sides against Dibble's legs, and licked the porter's dusty boots.

"Oh, this is the gent whose bin keind to yer, —eh, Mistress Momus?" said the man, nodding pleasantly to Dibble.

The dog gave a short bark, and rubbed herself once more against Dibble.

"Well, well, I forgives yer, Momus," said the man again, but this time in a softer voice, and with a coaxing kindliness which the dog seemed to understand.

"Come, then, old gal; stand up and make him

a bow," he went on, motioning to the dog with his hand.

Dibble's companion stood up as it had done in the corn-field, bowed gravely to Dibble, and raised a forepaw to its head, like charity school-boys on an inspection day.

"You've not fed the dawg too much, guvner," said the man, patting the dog's head, and addressing Dibble.

"I only saw un this afternoon," said Dibble, "for the first time, and I never see a dog so hungry and so quiet over it, nor one half so funny; I began to be afeared he wor something evil, he acted so much like a Christian, surely," said Dibble.

"Why, he's been away for this week or more —broken-hearted a'most; and we've bin obliged to fall back on the basket trick."

Thomas looked inquiringly at the little man, and wondered why showmen were so addicted to brown velveteen and pearl buttons.

"She can do pretty nigh everythin', can Momus;

she was the wife of a clown's dawg called Momus,
so we called her Mistress Momus. Everythin' she
can do pretty nigh, but like a brute I expected
her to do somethin' more nor everythin'; nothin'
would do but she must talk, and she couldn't
do that of course—no dawg could—and so we
quarrelled. Didn't we, old gal?"

The dog licked her master's hands, and looked
up into his face.

"I wanted her to say 'Thank 'e, sir.' Poor
lass, she tried hard, but she couldn't."

Mistress Momus here opened her mouth, and
jerked out something very much like "thank,"
and wagged her wretched stumpy tail.

"Never mind it, old gal; don't try agin," said
the master, patting the dog's head. "She couldn't
say 'Thank 'e, sir,' and I got savage and kicked
her, and druv her out, and threw a hammer at
her. Poor Momus! She's sulked before for a
day, but allers turned up for the evening per-
formances; but this time she's been out, as I was
a sayin', about a week—reglar done up, poor old

gal, and as thin as a skeleton. Why, you'd do to go with the human skeleton from Brummagem eh, old lass?—eh? They could get up a bit of special business for yer, eh, old wench?"

The dog barked, as if the notion was highly entertaining, and laid her head on the showman's knee.

"That's a new idea, isn't it, Momus," he went on; "but never mind, old gal, you shan't go on as a skeleton. Tip us a tumble, just to show you've got the free use of yer limbs, and then you shall have yer supper."

Momus turned a somersault, walked on her fore legs, danced on her hind legs, and then made another bow to Mr. Dibble; and that runaway conspirator was so diverted, that he forgot Mrs. Dibble and all his old friends, and called for another pint of beer.

The showman ordered in a dish of tripe, of which savoury meat the landlord had procured a large supply on the day previously for his expected customers; and Dibble, the dog, and an interesting young lady in faded silk and curls, were to be the showman's guests; the young lady being his daughter Christabel, as he informed Dibble, and one of the most rising gals of the day.

Supper was laid on a little round table near the fire-place, and an old pewter plate was placed on the floor for Momus.

"Give her all the scraps you've got, Dick," the showman said to the waiter, "and I'll come down 'ansum for it."

Dick brought in a variety of pickings, and heaped them upon the dish; Momus speedily devoured them, and then lay down beside the plate, at her master's request, "becos there was tripe to foller."

The tripe came in at length, hot and steaming, and floating about in a milky flood redolent of onions. A candle was placed in the middle of the table, and the showman held it over the brown dish for a moment to feast his eyes upon the contents, and then he dashed in a wooden

spoon and served out a plateful to Dibble and
his daughter, a few inches to Momus, and a large
quantity for himself. They all set-to with a
will, Christabel making short work with her
allowance, and helping herself to more, with
sudden rapidity. Her father cautioned her not
to be greedy. She only deigned to reply in one
word, the meaning of which, under the circumstances, seemed to be particularly significant; for
her father began to heap more tripe upon his own
plate, and Dibble began to ply his knife and
fork with increased rapidity. "Walker" was the
word which the fair Christabel had used with
such magic effect; but there was no necessity for
the alarm which it evidently created in her fond
parent's breast, seeing that she could not eat the
whole of that second lot, and the showman
and Dibble were not compelled to stint their
appetites.

After supper, the showman lighted a short
pipe, and ordered rum-and-water for three;
Christabel brought some mysterious article of

finery from her basket, and began to sew; and the three looked particularly happy and contented.

The showman drank Dibble's health, and then asked him what his little game might be.

Dibble drank the showman's health and the young lady's, and said he did not know what the showman meant.

"Gammon," said the showman. "Did yer 'ear that, Momus?"

Momus did not, for she was fast asleep at her master's feet.

"Ever been in the profession?" the showman inquired.

Dibble looked puzzled, and said "No."

"I mean the show business," said the man, blowing a cloud of smoke into the candlelight.

"No, I've been in different employ," said Dibble, feeling hot and comfortable with so much eating and drinking.

"Looking for work?"

"Yes," said Dibble.

" Would you like the show business?"

" Shouldn't mind anything to turn an honest penny," said Dibble.

"Well, as you've bin good to the dawg," said the showman, "I'll give you a few weeks' regler employment certain, though the season is getting to an end. I've been and invested in a horgan. I was afraid the dawg 'ud never come back, and I've added a horgan to the drum for the sake of hextra attraction on the outside. Would yer mind takin' the outside dooty and grindin' the horgan? I can give you a matter o' twelve shillin a week and most o' your grub."

Dibble said he was much obliged to the gentleman, and he would be glad to try his hand at the business; he could only give it up if he did not suit. So he was engaged on the spot, and became part of the establishment of " The Northern Magician," otherwise Digby Marquis, otherwise Bill Smith, the showman's real name.

The company consisted of himself and Chris-

tabel, who figured as "The Mysterious Lady,"
and the dog, who was known as "Madam Momus
the four-legged Wonder." They travelled with a
big cart-load of canvas, long poles, tressles, boards,
and boxes, drawn by two ancient horses remarkable for "high points," long necks, and drooping
heads.

They rose early the next morning and went on
their way over dusty high-roads, through green
shaded lanes covered with leaves, over country
bridges, and beneath railway viaducts. They
went on, now merrily down hill with cheery
words from Digby the showman, and now sadly
up hill with Dibble and Digby pushing behind,
and Christabel and Momus urging the horses in
front. Occasionally they rested beside green
patches of grass, and unlimbered the horses that
the poor brutes might crop the herbage. On
these occasions the showman smoked his pipe,
and gave Dibble bits of philosophical advice
anent his "outside dooties" in connection with
the organ and the drum.

Sometimes they travelled in company with cheap-jacks and peep-shows; but these were generally too swift of motion for Digby's establishment. Once a grand photographic saloon on radiant wheels, and with a smart young lady doing crochet work at the front door, went saucily by, without even a smile of contempt for the magician's poles and bundles and boxes. But Digby had a merry word for everybody, and Momus stood upon her hind-legs and made derisive bows now and then when the vehicles were particularly fast and showy.

At night, when the moon had risen, they arrived at the Severntown race-course, and Dibble sat down to rest, and wonder what Mrs. Dibble, Mr. Gibbs, and sundry other persons, thought about his running away.

CHAPTER XXIII.

IS OF A MISCELLANEOUS AND DISCURSIVE CHARACTER, BUT ESSENTIAL TO THE NARRATIVE.

"THE early bird for the worm," saith the proverb, which the healthy-wealthy-and-wise preachers quote with such stirring effect in the society of young people.

Supposing you are a bird, with an inordinate appetite for worms, it is good to rise early, no doubt; but if you are a worm it is better that you should not rise at the time when the early birds are congregated for breakfast.

Eight or nine o'clock is quite soon enough to begin the day if you have to begin it in misery; and if you have happiness before you all day long, you cannot get up too early to enjoy it.

Now Mrs. Dibble had a hard day before her, and not a particularly happy one, and she rose early at the call of duty; but she might just as well have had another hour's peaceful rest, for she was doomed to begin a day of more than ordinary trial.

Shuffleton Gibbs also rose earlier than usual on this eventful day, and it was well, for his own comfort, that he did do so, as a certain bird of very "taking" habits only found out his place of residence at a later hour of the morning, and would have demolished him had he not sneaked away from his customary locality an hour or so earlier.

So you see, whether we are birds or worms, we cannot count our chances of success or safety by our early rising. A certain worm may rise too early for the particular bird which is waiting for him, or he may lie abed just long enough to be snapped up by a late and luxurious cormorant; so, though the early bird may pick up the early worm, yet the lazy bird may also encounter the worm that is late.

The meaning of this is that proverbs are not necessarily the most truthful and useful things in the world, though Mrs. Dibble discovered some truth in the axiom, that "it can't rain but it pours."

A series of short, sharp screams were the earliest indications of something wrong in the Dibbleonian household on this morning of the "gude man's" departure.

Mrs. Dibble got up, as we have intimated, rather earlier than usual, for the purpose of preparing breakfast with her own hands, scorning to trust certain little delicacies of bacon and kidneys to her diminutive servant.

The sight of her extempore bed undisturbed and with no Thomas in it gave her a dreadful turn, as she explained afterwards, and that writing on the table with his confession in it might have knocked her down with a feather. So she screamed aloud, and as soon as she heard footsteps on the stairs she composed her morning gown into becoming folds, and posed herself for a comfortable faint upon the previously unpressed bed.

Mr. Somerton was the first to put in an appearance, then came Paul, and in a few minutes his sister Amy, all more or less frightened by Mrs. Dibble's screams. Mr. Somerton took the paper from her hands, read aloud the big open letters, and expressed his satisfaction in unmistakable language.

Amy threw her arms round Paul's neck, and at the same moment her father threw a jug of cold water into Mrs. Dibble's face, which roused that lady up in a fit of passion and indignation.

"Mithter Thomerton, thir, I wonder you are not ashamed of yourself, to treat a lady in that outdacious way, throwing a bucket of water over her as if she were a doorstep or some other inanimate thing, or one of your own cattle; but it's the way of the world,—oh, yes, nothing but ingratitude and all that's bad!"

Mrs. Dibble shook her dress, and wiped her face

with a towel, and shook her head, and stormed and stamped her feet, and gave other indications of perfect convalescence, and finally sank down again exhausted; but she sprang to her feet in an attitude of defence when Mr. Somerton seized the water-jug for the second time.

By-and-by the position of affairs was gravely discussed, and Mrs. Dibble talked of a hundred schemes of restoring Thomas to his home. She would send the police after him; she would advertise for him in the *Times*; she would follow him on foot through the wide wide world. Then in a moment of indignation she insisted upon his never returning to the roof which he had dis-honoured, and the harmonies of which would never go up to heaven any more on Sunday evenings as tokens of peace and honour. The old termagant grew quite eloquent in her distress and passion, and all the time expressed her con-viction that Paul was innocent as the lamb led to the slaughter.

The only thing which at all mollified her was

Amy's suggestion that perhaps poor Dibble had been tempted to do wrong because he loved his wife so dearly; though Mrs. Dibble insisted that it was not love she valued so highly as honour and virtue and prudence, however much she had certainly been attached to Thomas in the early days of their courtship.

Things were assuming, it will be seen, rather a ridiculous aspect when Mr. Williamson arrived, with his grave, amiable face, to put affairs upon a proper footing. He mastered Dibble's confession immediately, and rubbed his hands over it and smiled.

"Yes, yes," he said, "we must change places to-day, Paul; we must put you in the witness-box, and Gibbs in the dock: that will be a good joke, eh? It's really a capital case—as nice a bit of conspiracy as could well be imagined. I thought yours was an honest face, young man," he continued, addressing Paul, "as soon as you appeared."

Paul blushed, and said, "Thank you, Mr. Williamson."

The journalist and barrister then made a quiet effort to learn from Paul his reasons for taking such an interest in the doings of Mr. Gibbs at the Ashford Club.

Paul hesitated and looked at his sister, who immediately came to his assistance.

"I induced Paul to make inquiries," she said.

Her father and the rest looking for some further observation, she said,

"Paul heard some strange things, concerning Mr. Tallant's son, and—and Mr. Hammerton, who resided near us. I was anxious, if possible, to learn the truth of the rumours, which were to their discredit. In truth, it seemed as though the good name and reputation of Mr. Hammerton were likely to be lost to him, as if he were being gradually led into the society of disreputable people and deceived, and——"

Amy was very much at fault in her attempted explanation; she felt that she hardly knew why she had interfered, now that she endeavoured to justify it. Curiosity, excited by Paul's letters, had been her first impulse, and then her romantic love for Hammerton had shown her the danger into which he was drifting. . Her hero a gambler, the man whom she held up in her imagination as the best and the truest and purest and noblest, an associate of gamblers and speculators and drunkards ; the idea had tortured her to an extent quite sufficient to add eloquent point to her inquiries concerning Hammerton and Tallant, which had at first puzzled Paul, and then enlisted him in her service as Mr. Hammerton's good angel.

Could she explain this, with the eyes of her father and Mr. Williamson upon her ? She succeeded in leaving on the mind of the latter gentlemen the impression that she had had a mind to pry into the private doings of these gentlemen from idle girlish curiosity, and that Paul had been very foolish in giving way to her; but Mr. Somerton saw a little further than this into the secret of his daughter.

"Well, we must not stay chatting here," said Mr. Williamson at length; "I will go and apply

for a warrant against this Mr. Gibbs for conspiracy; and with regard to your husband, Mrs.
Dibble, you had better take no steps at present
to discover him."

Mrs. Dibble, who had been mechanically lighting the fire and boiling the kettle all this time,
turned round and requested Mr. Williamson to
attend to his own business, and promised the
whole company that she would attend to hers.

Upon this Mr. Williamson declined the lady's
invitation to breakfast, and went away in company
with Paul, whom Mr. Somerton and his daughter
promised to meet at Bow Street at twelve o'clock,
when Paul's bail expired.

A warrant for conspiracy was granted against
Mr. Shuffleton Gibbs; but nearly an hour before
a detective from Scotland Yard tapped at Mr.
Gibbs' door to execute the warrant, his land-
lady had slipped inside her lodger's bed-room the
rough-looking note of Dibble's. It happened that
Mr. Gibbs rose a little earlier that morning, or
he would not have received the warning in time

to have taken measures for his own safety. As it was, he no sooner received the letter than he commenced to prepare for flight.

In the midst of a volley of "curses not loud but deep," he deposited a few articles of linen and other things in a valise, into which he emptied the contents of a small cash-box. Then from a drawer beneath the bedstead he brought forth a grey wig, a long strait coat, and a pair of green spectacles.

"Somehow I thought I should come to this at last," he said, tossing the things upon the bed and locking the bed-room door. "The luck's against me."

And then he swore bitterly, and savagely ground his teeth, and coughed, and vowed the direst vengeance against everybody.

Taking up a pair of scissors, he cut off his whiskers and moustaches, and wrapped them up in paper.

"I must burn them somehow," he said to himself. "What an ass I must be to get myself into this mess to satisfy my revenge on a boy,—a twopenny-halfpenny clerk whom I ought to have thrashed within an inch of his life."

He went on muttering to himself as he shaved his face clean and bare. He certainly was not improved by the operation. The bad lines about his mouth came out in painful distinctness, now that the hair was gone.

Fastening a white band about his neck, Mr. Gibbs next adjusted the grey wig upon the partially bald head, put on the green spectacles, donned the long strait coat, opened his bed-room door, listened attentively for a moment, and then quietly disappeared down-stairs and out at the front.

He had an hour's start of the police, and he maintained his advantage cleverly.

No prosecutor appeared at Bow Street against Paul, and the purse was impounded,—"rather a sell for Mr. Gibbs that," as Williamson said in his quiet amiable way afterwards. The magistrate said Paul left that court an injured young man, without a blemish on his character.

In the evening Amy and her father returned home, and they would fain have had Paul's company; but Mr. Williamson begged that they would let Paul spend the evening with him, as he thought he could introduce the lad to a better situation than the one at Westminster.

Amy looked the gratitude which she felt for Mr. Williamson's great kindness, and Mr. Somerton delicately pressed a ten-pound note upon him just "to buy something, you know, in remembrance of the affair—not in the way of payment for a moment, but to buy a ring or something as a token of a father's gratitude for protecting his son when no friends were near."

Mr. Williamson could not resist the fine fellow, as he said at the Club afterwards, "there was something so noble in the way in which it was done. A true son of the soil that Somerton—a

fine noble fellow with his heart in his eyes, and
then his splendid daughter standing by and
looking so appealingly, by Jove, I took the note,
and the young fellow and I went together into
Regent Street and spent it."

This Club of which we speak was the Cavendish,
—a Club frequented by artists, actors, writers for
magazines, and newspaper critics,—and in the
evening, Mr. Williamson, one of its most lovable
members, introduced his *protégé* Paul.

It represented quite a new world to the bailiff's
son,—and a world which was highly attractive.
A new drama had been produced on this evening,
and soon after eleven o'clock quite a small crowd
of fellows came in to eat chops, drink grog, and
discuss the new play.   Some of them shook
hands with Williamson, called him "dear boy,"
and asked what new bit of philanthropy he had
in hand.   He introduced Paul to one gentleman
as his *amicus curiæ*, his *camarade*, his *fidus
Achates*, and said he wished to recommend Paul
to him for a clerkship in his office.

"I know you have a vacancy, because I inquired yesterday. Read the papers to-morrow about a case at Bow Street—the one in which I was engaged,—they were talking about it here, you know, last night,—don't ask any questions, but wait until I call upon you to-morrow."

"All right," old fellow," said the gentleman ; and when he had joined a companion at the furthest end of the room, Mr. Williamson said, "That gentleman is the proprietor of *The Pyrotechnic*, a musical, theatrical, and literary paper of which, *entre nous*, I am the editor."

Paul during the whole night acted upon the nursery proverb—listened and said nothing. He heard all sorts of wonderful things about dramatic art and literary criticism, and Mr. Williamson pointed out to him the most notable personages present. One of the quietest and "meekest-minded" fellows there was the leading low comedian of a famous theatre ; and the noisiest and funniest dog of the lot was the gentleman who played high tragic characters at the same house. The most "disputatious person" was a musician who talked of German operas and the unities of the classic drama. A gentleman who was renowned as a wit spoke of the gorgeous poetic beauty of the Psalms; and a preacher who contributed leading articles to a popular religious paper got a little applause and some quiet expressions of irony by designating himself "a professor of Hebrew mythology."

Paul did not quite understand this latter bit of smart profanity at the time; but he learnt eventually to estimate it at its true value, and understand how much of the practical unbelief of the day arises from the want of downright earnestness on the part of many professed religious teachers. Mr. Williamson often talked about questions of this character with Paul in after days at his quiet chambers in the Temple, and Paul found at the bottom of Williamson's philanthropy a fine vein of religious feeling. And yet Mr. Williamson was a disappointed man. The world had not gone well with him, he used to say. He commenced life with grand theories and sentiments, and with convictions too strong, and a heart too suscep- tible of honour and truth and honesty, to let him register vows which he did not feel that he could perform to the letter. Otherwise he might have been a shining light perchance in the Church : at all events he would have been true to her, not like that miserable fellow who talked about Hebrew mythology, and chuckled over his own infamy. Mr. Williamson had avoided this re- ligious writer ever afterwards ; not, as he said, for being an unbeliever, not because he was an atheist, but because he belonged to the holiest and best of all professions and made a boast of his perjury and unfaithfulness. Mr. Williamson gave the greatest latitude to free-thinking, and never interfered in religious controversies, and he instilled into Paul's mind opinions of libe- rality and toleration.

It was strange that Williamson should have

taken such a fancy to Paul Somerton ; but he was an eccentric, amiable, kindly fellow, and his ways and mode of life, his likes and dislikes, his selection of companions, and his general motives of action were not influenced by common impulses : he had habits of thought and ways of his own, and he took it into his head that he would help this young fellow whom Fortune had thrown in his way.

CHAPTER XXIV.

CHRISTABEL TAKES DIBBLE INTO HER CONFIDENCE.

THOUGH Thomas Dibble never, during all his connection with "The Temple of Magic," had seen a performance from beginning to end, he had seen enough to surprise and delight him, and whenever an opportunity offered, he communicated to Christabel the feelings of wonder with which he regarded her.

" You be certainly the cleverest lady as ever I see," said Thomas, one night after business, as the pair sat alone over supper, in a corner of the general room of the lodging-house where the magician's company were quartered. The renowned Digby had gone out to a lamb's fry supper given in honour of the birth-day of the Yorkshire giant, whose acquaintance he had recently made.

" Do you think so ? " said the amiable young lady, looking all kinds of sweet things at Dibble. " Ah, I might have been, if poor old Carkey had lived."

" It would hardly be possible for you to be any cleverer," said Dibble. " However you does change them cards so wonderful, is a mystery to me."

" Ah, that's easy enough, Thomas ; I mean clever at reading and writing, and all that. You didn't know Carkey, of course. He was father's clown. Ah, these were the days ! We once had a circus company, Thomas ; a real grand affair, with horses, and ladies in spangles and tights, and father used to stand in the middle in jackboots and crack a whip."

" You don't say so ! " said Dibble, who felt highly honoured at the condescension of the young lady in telling him all this.

" O, yes ; it was stunning, I can tell you. I was a very little girl at the time—very little ; I can only just remember it ; but Carkey, the clown, when father was done up, and had to turn to conjuring, he stuck to us for long enough, and it was he who used to tell me all about it."

" I never see a clown but once," said Dibble, "and that was when me and——"

" Yes," said Christabel, " you and——"

" Well, I was going to say," Dibble stammered.

" You and——" repeated Christabel. " Now, you are keeping something from me : if it's a secret, tell it me, and I'll tell you another— such a first-rater."

" You will ?" exclaimed Dibble.

" Yes," said Christabel, nodding her head, and laughing quite gleefully.

" And you'll never tell, on your blessed oath ?" said Dibble. " But what's the good of oaths ? I'd rather trust to your honour."

" Then you may," said Christabel; "for I'm longing to tell you a secret,—one that I've kept for, O, ever so long ! Now, who was it when you and——"

" Well, then, I wor going to say, when me and

Mrs. Dibble—which be my wife," said Thomas, " once went to a pantomime, and see the clown eat three yards of sausages, and jump through a clock."

" So you've a wife ? " said Christabel, disregarding altogether the wonderful feat of the clown in the pantomime.

" Yes ; and I've bin and run away from her," said Dibble ; " so there's my secret, and I trusts to your honour."

" What did you run away for ? " asked Christabel.

" Well, 'cos I'd bin and got into trouble in the panic," said Dibble.

" What's a panic ? " asked Christabel. " I never heard of a panic."

" Why, you see, it's a sort of row in the City about what shares be worth, and which buys 'em, and who sells 'em, and whether you've got 'em, or the other one ; but the great thing of all is to know what a bull is, and which is the bear, and whether you ought to be one or the 'tother, and whether it's premium or par, or what the discount be."

This was one of the longest explanatory speeches that Dibble had ever made, except when he was trying to convince Mrs. Dibble that he was a bull, and could not help it. He looked at Christabel, and fancied that he had given a particularly lucid description of a panic; but the mysterious lady stared in astonishment at Dibblé, and said—

" So that's a panic, is it ? "

" Yes it be, summat near it," said Dibble. " I ought to know, considerin' as I lost five hundred pounds in it."

Dibble raised his head, and looked quite important when he thought of his financial experience.

" Well I never heard of a panic before," said Christabel. "I begun to think you must be going off your head—' off your nut,' as father calls it— when you talked of bears and bulls, or else that a panic was a menagerie, and you really had been in the profession before."

" No, a panic bain't a menagerie," said Dibble ;
" it's worse nor anything of that sort ; it's something as you can't see, but it's got a way of
getting at your money, and swallering of it up in
the most outdacious style, and the more it gets,
the more you has to give it."

" Why, it must be a menagerie," said Christabel.

" What be a menagerie,—wild beasts ? "

" Of course, you know that," said Christabel, a
little impatiently.

" Well, it's worse than the awfullest wild beasts
as ever you heard on ; but you can't see it. I
thought you could myself, and I went into the
City and inquired. ' Where be the panic ? ' I says
to a porter as I knowed. ' In there,' says he,
' in the Stock Exchange.' I looked into a place,
through a hole, and there I sees above a hundred
men, a talking, and shouting, and writing in little
books, and going on like Bedlam ; but I never see
the panic. So I asks a man as was standing close
by, and he begun to laugh and told me to inquire
of a fat party again the door, and he said I was to

ask the Old Woman of Threadneedle-street. I went there, and I see an old 'oman, a selling oranges, which I asked at once. She said she thought that was it, pointing to a great big house; but I never see it, and I 'eard arter, as it was not to be seen, that it was like the devil going about in the character of a roaring lion on the quiet, never letting anybody see 'un."

Dibble was becoming quite garrulous upon the panic, and Christabel sat looking at him with a startled sort of curiosity; she had never heard of such a wonderful animal before; but then, she said, there were no doubt many things of which she was ignorant.

"If Carkey had lived," she went on, "I should have known all about everything, because he said he would teach me, and some day he said I might become a fine lady.   Just fancy, wouldn't that be fizzing, to be a fine lady ! If I was to tell your secret, you'd be in an awful way, eh ? It would be a reglar do, wouldn't it ? "

"Hawful," said Dibble.

" That's right, 'cause I want to tell you mine. Now, look here."

Christabel looked cautiously round, to see if the miscellaneous company were occupied. Convinced that nobody was watching them, she took from her bosom a small miniature.

" Now, you see that ? " she said, in a whisper.

" Yes," said Dibble, fully expecting to see it changed into a pigeon or something more wonderful still, in the way of conjuring.

" That is the picture of a lady. Carkey gave it to me, and he told me never to part with it for love or money. It is a picture of a real lady, such a beauty, and he says,—you swear you will never split ? "

" Never," said Dibble, solemnly.

" Well, that this lady was my mother, and that my father was a gentleman ; that Digby Martin is not my father at all, and that some day I would perhaps find out my real father. I promised on his death-bed always to call Digby father, and never to let anything make me not do so, and that I was to try and learn things out of books, and read newspapers, and all that. Now, I've always wanted somebody to talk to since poor Carkey died, and to ask their opinion about it; and now you and I shall be friends for ever,—eh, Thomas?"

"Oh, yes, sure," said Dibble. "I wouldn't tell your secret for all the world. What a wonderful girl you be, surely!"

"Ain't I?" said Christabel, quite proudly. "I often thinks of it when I'm going through the performance, and especially lately. I read in bed, and sometimes of a morning; and I know it's true what Carkey said, because there's a tale just like it in the paper which I buy every Saturday morning, as sure as the day comes round; and O, it makes my blood boil! O, it's such a fizzing story, and there's pictures of her in it! She was stolen by gipsies, and they made her sell buy-a-brooms and matches; and she was a lord's daughter all the time! And who knows, Thomas, but that I am the same?

Haven't I got a picture in my bosom, and all that? O, wouldn't I go it if I ever came to be rich! And I mean to be, Dibble; I'm not a-going to be always performing here, don't think it!"

Dibble said Miss Christabel ought to be in London, at the British Museum, or somewhere.

When she knew a little more of things in general, Christabel said she meant to try her fortune. There were lots of marriages in the tale she was reading, and always a lot in the newspapers. Why shouldn't she be married?

" Why, you be too young for that," said Dibble. " I know a young gentleman as would make such a sweetheart for you," said Dibble; "such a sweetheart!"

" Yes," said Christabel, smiling her sweetest, and putting her hair to rights.

" But there, he be miles and miles away from here," said Dibble; "and you're never likely to see him, Ise afeared."

" What is he like ? " said Christabel, preparing for a flirtation in fancy.

"O, a handsome, nice young gentleman; and his name's Paul."

" What a jolly, stunning name ! " said Christabel.

" He wouldn't like you to speak like that," said Dibble.

" How do you mean ? " asked Christabel.

" Why stunning and all that—it bain't perlite; he talks so fine himself, he do."

" I know what you mean," said the young lady. " I can talk fine, too. I know stunning isn't fine; but I know what is, so there !"

" You bain't angry now ? " said Dibble.

" Not at all — oh, no," said Christabel. " What's his other name ? "

" Somerton," said Dibble. " Master Paul Somerton."

" Oh ! and do you think he would fall in love with me ? "

" I should think he would," said Dibble, as-

tonished that there should be any opening for
doubt upon the subject.

"Oh, how nice! I often think some grand
young gentleman will come into the Temple
and fall in love with me; but I never see a
real handsome one come in, dressed pretty, you
know, and with a little moustache, like the
pictures in the tale that I was telling you of.
I always looks round the audience to see if
there is aireyone as is in love with me; aireyone as I could love, you know. But they are all
such a gawky lot. Most of them are in love
with me—I know that, of course; but they
are hardly worth being made miserable. O, I
gives them such looks sometimes!"

Christabel seemed to hug herself upon her
assumed capacity to make some of the male
portion of her audiences unhappily in love with
her, and Dibble felt morally certain that it
would be impossible for any young gentleman
not to fall in love with her; but as for
marriage it was nonsense, Dibble told her, to

think of that,—such a very young lady as she was; he should think for his part that she ought to be able to conjure some handsome young gentleman into that basket when she disappeared at the touch of her father's wand— disappeared nobody knew where. But the young lady only laughed at this, and thought it a good joke.

What if she could conjure into it that handsome Paul Somerton, she said, who talked so fine!

Dibble said that would be splendid, and then Christabel as a further proof of her favour, gave Thomas her royal permission to call her "Chrissy." Carkey, the clown, had always called her "Chrissy," and in future Dibble should take the clown's place, and be her confidant.

"But mind," she said, clenching her little hand, "if you dare to betray me—if you do not keep my secret,—I will not only tell yours, but oh, I don't know what I will not do besides— shoot you, perhaps, with a pistol, like the lord's daughter in the tale."

Christabel said this so fiercely that Dibble almost wished she had not confided her secret to him. Just as he was about to make a remark to this effect, there staggered into the room, reeling through the smoke, the showman and his "dawg." The company hammered their glasses on the tables and shouted "bravo," as Digby strutted in with the Yorkshire giant and Momus, the giant smiling benignly upon his tipsy friend, and Momus marching in front with her head very erect, and her nose turned towards her proprietor.

Thomas Dibble had hardly raised his eyes to look at his new master and the giant, when Digby seized a cup and threw it at Momus, and, missing his mark, made stupid efforts to kick the animal, whereupon Christabel rushed to the dog's rescue and called the showman a brute, at which there was another burst of applause. The giant hereupon lifted Digby up by his collar out of harm's way, as if in terrible affright at Christabel; at this Digby kicked and swore, and the giant, dropping him, said the young lady was right, Digby Martin was indeed a brute; and it was generally agreed that this was the most courageous thing that a giant had ever been known to do and say. This led to a dispute between a very tall gentleman in the peep-show line, and the proprietor of a boxing booth, which ended in an extempore fight on the spot; in the midst of which Christabel retired in disgust, quietly intimating to Dibble that she would not put up with "this sort of thing" much longer. Dibble slunk away too, and wished there had never been such a thing as a panic in the City.

END OF VOL. I.

BRADBURY, EVANS, AND CO., PRINTERS, WHITEFRIARS.

www.ingramcontent.com/pod-product-compliance
Lightning Source LLC
Chambersburg PA
CBHW020846020726
47497CB00005B/1276